a heart's war

THE BROKEN MEN CHRONICLES

book five

carey decevito

DEDICATION

For those who give so much of themselves in their everyday life. Although your efforts may seem thankless more often than not, remember that the impact you've had in shaping someone's tomorrow will never go unnoticed.

ACKNOWLEDGMENTS

I can't believe this series has reached its end! I can honestly say that I wouldn't have been able to achieve this milestone were it not for the amazing team of people I've surrounded myself with over the course of this past year.

Eric David Battershell, has it already been five covers already? Thank you for sharing your art with the world. Your talent with the camera, your dedication and your friendship has meant so much more than you'll ever know. I can't wait for us to jump on our next adventure together. Believe me, there will be more!

Clarise Tan, your attention to detail, the way you've taken Eric's shots of the guys and masterly worked them for this series has been amazing. We've had so many laughs and I love your zest for the work that you do. Girl, you'll always be my go-to person for my covers. My dear sister from another mother, I can't wait to see what we come up with next.

Stefan Northfield, you've been absolutely amazing to work with. Thank you for your support, your kind words and encouragement. When I looked through thousands of images to find what I needed for this book's cover, I never expected for your image to inspire Theo's journey like it has.

To Marisa Caldwell, Laurie Cooper and the Pub-Craft team, you guys have been a force to be reckoned with. Thank you for being there when needed, and sometimes on short notice. Whenever I need a hand with something, whether it be advertising, editing, a book tour, or any random task I just can't seem to find the time for, you guys are there for me.

My dearest readers, words seem insufficient to express my appreciation your loyalty and support for this series in particular. This may be the end to *The Broken Men Chronicles* but rest assured, this isn't the last you'll be reading from me! Thank you for your readership, your kind words, and constructive feedback.

And last but certainly not least, I owe a debt of gratitude to my husband and our two daughters. Without your love, your patience and understanding, I wouldn't be where I am today. I love you all so very much, and thank you for allowing me to pursue a long-wished for dream. You're my love, my life, my inspiration.

PROLOGUE

A fiery blast came from our left. The vehicle I was crammed into took a sharp right before weightlessness set in; the deafening sound of crunching metal, shattering glass, and firing weapons making my ears ring. My head felt as if it was about to explode.

Shouts, screams from the men around me, those I was responsible for, their sounds were what living nightmares were made of.

Suspended for eternity is how it felt when in fact, within seconds it was over.

"Donnelly," I coughed out, stuck sideways against my door. My vision was blurry, my head pounding. Everything was tinged with red. "Donnelly," I repeated, chocking on the dust and smoke floating inside the vehicle. I tried wiping blood from my eyes. Whether it was mine or someone else's, I couldn't tell. When I got nothing from Donnelly, I addressed the group. "Everyone okay?"

No answer.

I blinked a few times, the ringing in my ears dying down enough for me to be able to make out the horrific chaos that surrounded us outside. The erratic thumping in my chest, not to mention the prickling of the small hairs on the back of my neck, told me that danger still lurked.

I hoped that our Humvee was the only one in our convoy that had been hit, but with the size of that blast, I knew it was wishful thinking. We needed to get out, help whoever was left, and get the hell back to base.

I tried to move, biting my lip hard enough to taste the coppery flavor of my own blood as the debilitating pain in my legs manifested itself, letting me know that I was in bad shape.

"Damon." I leaned forward as much as I could, trying to get around his seat without blacking out, to rouse my teammate, one of my best friends. It wasn't until my eyes were firmly focused on him that I noticed his head hanging at an unnatural angle, his chest unmoving. I reached as far as I could, finding that spot by his carotid to make sure what I was seeing was right. My rations from that morning's breakfast began to weigh heavy and my gut clenched, bile beginning to rise, when I had my confirmation. "Oh fuck!"

The man lay against what should have been the window to his door—dead.

Beside him, the newest addition to our team—a woman we'd dubbed Tiny, for evident reasons—lay across the middle console, aortic blood spraying lightly as the last of her life force drained away.

Blood. There was so much of it. Keeping my sanity in check became harder as panic consumed me.

I can't be all that's left. I can't be alone in this hell.

So I turned to the last of my team members: Rick Donnelly. Just like with Damon, we'd been close, he and I. A true brother in this godforsaken sandbox, who'd kept me level-headed throughout our many deployments since BUD/S. He's a little crazy, but I suppose that's why he's a master with explosives.

"Rick!" At first glance, Donnelly appeared unharmed, as if he were sleeping. The sweet sound of his groan cut through the automatic gunfire around us enough to dispel my ever-growing sense of helplessness. Barely.

The sudden lull in weapon fire provided me with the opportunity to call his name out again. I knew insurgents were still around and we needed to get gone fast.

As I tried to rouse Donnelly, I became aware of approaching footsteps. I prayed for it to be our men but I knew that in all likelihood we might not be so lucky. The radio silence alluded to that fact.

"Dammit, Rick, wake the fuck up! We need to get out of here."

The man managed another groan but didn't move despite my grabbing on to his fatigues and shaking him.

I heard shouts outside our vehicle; both English and foreign. Just as another bout of gunfire hit, the distinctive sound of our M-16's against AK-47's, everything drew to a halt. The sound of gurgling close to the rear of our vehicle and the rapid fire of Pashto sent me into a full-blown panic. This felt too much like the end.

Seconds later, I was ripped from my seat, the searing pain in my legs escalating to a blinding level, making me scream.

As soon as two men laid hands on Rick, he kicked into action.

Fully extricated and now able to better see my surroundings, I heard weapons still firing intermittently in the distance, screams and pleas of mercy came from all directions, none of them in my native tongue though.

I tried to fight my captors but the injury to my legs had me useless against the two able-bodied men that held me. Before I knew it, my hands and ankles were bound with rope, a gag was shoved into my mouth, tied by a torn piece of cloth, and an old rice bag that smelled of sweat and mildew was slipped over my head.

In this moment, thoughts of my future, my family, my friends flashed through my mind. If I survived this ambush I knew before long, I'd be praying for death. I just didn't know how right I would be.

With a hit to the back of my head I fell into darkness.

CHAPTER 1

"Welcome to Jacksonville, North Carolina, folks! The current temperature…" The flight attendant's voice startles me awake from my flashback. My breathing is erratic, my skin is crawling and clammy as I force myself to take in my surroundings and calm myself. Suffice to say, my nightmares were back. If I'm being honest, they hadn't really disappeared. But, with my imminent return home, they'd grown in frequency.

The elderly lady sitting next to me cowered in the furthest corner of her seat, her eyes wide, face pale. Her expression of fear morphed to one of sympathy as she eyed my fatigues, evidently processing my attire along with my behavior as soon as "I'm sorry," had left my mouth. Patting my arm, she turned to face forward without a word. It's too bad there weren't more people like her. I didn't need anyone claiming to understand what I'd been through. I didn't need their pity. And I certainly didn't need their praise and thanks.

I hadn't been home in ten years. Half of that time hadn't been by choice, either. I had owed it to my country to serve with distinction. Or, that's what I'd believed at one time.

A hero is what most everyone dubs me. The thought itself makes me cringe. Where's the honour, the glory, even the pride in it? Did anyone who killed, who witnessed death in all its violent forms, who slept every night with one eye open, wondering if they'd live to see the next day, think of themselves a hero? I can't speak for anyone else but the short answer for me is no.

Grabbing my rucksack, I head for the exit. The flight attendant sends a flirtatious smile my way. "Have an enjoyable stay, sir." I walked off the plane with only a curt nod as an acknowledgment.

After a quick stop at luggage claim, I exit the airport with nothing but my rucksack and a large duffle strewn over my shoulder, words of praise from passers-by having fallen on deaf ears. The pats on the back made me want to shrink away. It all made me want to scream, but those that haven't been where I've been, that haven't done what I've done, or seen what I've seen didn't know any better, did they? They held on to this romanticised version of what the media portrayed. If they only knew that the boogey man came in the form of a man, woman, or child and not with pins sticking out of their heads, or blades for fingers.

No, there was no glory in being considered a hero for my country. Those considered heroes in my book are the ones who fought and lost their lives, that have made the ultimate sacrifice. Those who were now six feet under, if their families were lucky enough to have a piece of their loved ones shipped back to them for a proper farewell.

My scars, both physical and emotional, run deeper than they appear. They serve as a reminder of those I've lost in the line of duty, those I had been in charge of, sworn to protect and bring back to their families. Alive. Those I had failed.

I hailed a cab and jumped in as soon as one pulled up in front of me.

"Where to?"

I don't know, home? Where the hell was home, really? Everyone thought I was dead.

"Hey buddy," the driver said. "Did you hear me?"

"Is there a bar around here? I'd kill for a cold beer and a decent burger."

"I know just the place." The mid-fifties man's eyes crinkled in the mirror.

Despite the curious looks the driver threw my way, the drive was made in silence and I was grateful. As the tree-lined streets and lights from oncoming traffic whizzed by, I found myself thinking about a plan of attack to reintegrate myself into what most people would call a normal life.

By the time the taxi pulled up to the curb, I still had no idea how to approach the situation that was my return from the dead. Perhaps my answers lay at the bottom of a beer bottle too many, or better yet, with my brother. He'd always been one to help me think things through in a rational and practical fashion.

But how will P take it?

I stood with my two bags, a summary of my life for the past decade, staring up at the pub in front of me. Fairfax. The place seemed fairly new. I didn't recall seeing it before leaving, that's for sure.

The sound of laughter, the smell of food and liquor assaulted me as I opened the door. The place appeared pretty quiet for a Friday night. It was just what I needed.

Starting toward the bar, I heard, "Son of a bitch!" making me freeze mid-stride. It might have been a little more than three years since, but that voice was one I'd never forget.

My head turned in the speaker's direction, the place having gone dead silent. A man came barrelling toward me, a flying fist connecting with my jaw before I could shield myself. My body rocked backward as I dropped my bags in shock.

"What the fuck are you doing here?" Paxton demanded. "You're supposed to be dead!"

Not exactly the homecoming I was expecting.

"Good to see you too, bro." I rubbed my jaw. *Fuck that hurt.*

Before I knew it, Paxton was on top of me, swinging like a mad man, yelling, cursing me out until I was forced to defend myself. Couldn't a guy catch a break? Couldn't I have at least had the chance to explain?

I was pushed onto a table, which collapsed, causing my brother and I to fall in a pile of splintered rubble to the floor.

"You just left!" Paxton landed a punch to my gut, knocking the wind out of me.

"I didn't have a choice!" I shouted back, blocking a hit before rolling us over so I was on top. I managed to get to my feet, swiping the back of my hand over my split lip to check for bleeding as I braced myself for another go, if that's what he wanted.

"Get the fuck out of here!" My brother picked himself off the floor, then came at me again.

I landed a hit to his jaw and another to his stomach. "I just got back and that's all you have to say? The least I deserve is a chance to explain."

We thought we buried you!

My brother's words sent reality crashing through me. I hadn't forgotten about the heartbreaking news that had been delivered to my friends and family what felt like a lifetime ago. No one forgets that. But then again, I never gave thought about how my sudden reappearance would be taken either.

Next thing I knew, Paxton was being held back from another approach, and so was I.

When my breathing calmed, I said, "I'm cool," to the guys who had me restrained. Their grips loosened to release me altogether.

"What happened to you, man?" I recognized the guy on my left as Ben Carpenter.

Shaking my head in response, I rubbed the back of my neck, peering down at the floor before meeting Ben and my brother's gazes. Everyone seemed to have calmed down, but they were also awaiting my answer.

So I relayed my story. Well, the bits I could share, anyway. I told them about our ambush, how I had been captured, wished I had died, but had survived instead. When it came down to why no one was told that I was alive and well, I didn't have much in the way of an explanation because everything was classified to the nth degree. "It would have been too risky for everyone. You have no—"

"Don't tell me I have no idea!" Paxton spat. "*You* have no idea of the shit we've been through."

"Pax!" A woman came to stand beside him, her hands on his chest. According to the information that I'd been able to dig up, I knew this was Alissa, my brother's wife…and my new sister-in-law.

"Don't!" The pained look on his face had her eyes tearing up. "His own nephew nearly died and he wasn't here. He hasn't even met his niece. He knows nothing of our lives and he expects us to welcome him back with open arms?" Paxton's eyes bore into me. The betrayal they held was like a searing knife to the heart. "You deserted me!"

After a moment, I managed to choke down the ball of emotions that clogged my throat. "I knew."

His eyes widened. "What?"

Our gazes remained locked. "I said I *knew*. I know that you and Julie didn't work out…about the divorce. I know what happened with Jasper, Alissa coming into your life, and when that beautiful little princess of yours was born. Just because I didn't stay in touch doesn't mean I don't care. I've kept tabs on my family the entire time I was away because that's the only thing I could do. I don't think I would have survived if I hadn't been able to do that."

The look of shock and relief in my brother's eyes filled me with hope. "As messed up as this all is, I believe you." He sighed, pinching the bridge of his nose between his thumb and forefinger as if trying to rid himself of a sudden headache. "I need a drink after this bombshell. Want one?"

That classic Lowell grin spread onto his face before he took his wife's hand and led her toward the bar. "It's the least I can do for that busted lip. When did your face get so hard?"

I chuckled, falling into step beside them. *Same old P.* I was glad he hadn't changed. "Training." I patted him on the back. "By the way, your left hook could use some work, it's weak."

"Two Jack's and a raspberry martini for my wife, Derek." Alissa curled into Paxton's side as he eyed my face, that sure-of-himself grin still present. "Let me know if I still need practice when that jaw barely opens tomorrow and you can't see out of your right eye."

CHAPTER 2

Only when Paxton headed toward the men's room with his wife did I swivel my barstool and look around. I felt like a fly on the wall, content to observe the festivities without partaking in them, recognizing a few faces, most of them from high school, while others were new.

Earlier, my brother brought up a few points that had me thinking. I needed to see my parents. I needed a job. And my younger sibling also saw it fit to tell me that I needed a woman.

Well, I couldn't agree more with the first two, but the last one was debatable.

To be honest, I don't want a night of hot fun where I sink my cock in some willing stranger. To have that would be like never having evolved from my old ways. And I wasn't the old Theo Lowell. Far from it, in fact. I wanted a simple life with a partner—much like my brother and his friends seem to have acquired, if tonight was anything to go by. What I wanted was a woman to call my own.

No one will have you once they know everything.

That pesky internal voice was always there, reminding me of the things I have done, or better yet, the things I failed to do during my deployments, things that no woman would overlook for the kind of long haul commitment I yearned for.

"Just as well," I said to myself as I tilted the remainder of my beer back.

Cat calls and hollers sounded from the area where the

gents and ladies' rooms were located. I turned to see what the women were going on about to find none other than my brother blushing while the women high-fived his wife.

Derek waved another bottle of *Bud Light* at me and I nodded. Catching wind of what had gone on had me smirking as I took a large gulp of my fresh brew. I guess my brother had finally found himself someone to keep up with his wilder side after that frigid bitch of an ex he'd been married to had left him.

Alissa settled herself on the stool next to mine having left Paxton to deal with the guys razing him.

"So, Theo," she eyed me, "where are you spending the night?"

"I was thinking of the Sunset Inn on Western Boulevard."

I was met with a disapproving look. "I'm not going to let you hole yourself up in a hotel when we have a perfectly well-made-up room at the house."

I harrumphed. "That tiny townhouse only has two rooms."

Paxton nudged my shoulder with his as he leaned against the bar on my other side. "We're living in Mom and Dad's old place now."

"The ranch?" Alissa nodded. Something inside me ached to see the old place again. "You're sure?" I knew that it would be fine with my brother, so I aimed my gaze at his better half, who nodded once more. "Okay. Thank you."

The look of approval in my brother's eyes told me that accepting his wife's invitation had been the right move.

CHAPTER 3

The next morning, I woke to two wide piercing blue eyes staring back at me.

"Wow," the kid said, "you're big!"

Chuckling, I ruffled his hair as I sat up. "You've gotten bigger too, buddy."

His eyes lost a bit of their glimmer as they took on a hesitant look. "Are you really my uncle Theo?"

Smiling to help reassure the kid, I said, "Sure am."

The kid threw himself into my arms with a vice-like hug. "You look different. How come we haven't seen you on the computer for so long?" I may have not been home in a decade, but I had kept in touch all the way up until my capture. With *all* of them, my father being the exception.

"Top secret, Jasp."

"Like spy stuff?" I set him on his feet, his grin making me chuckle.

"More like super spy stuff." I nudged his chin with my fist.

"Oooh!" His excitement was palpable. "Are you back to stay or just to visit?"

He looked as if his world would end if I didn't provide him with the right answer, so I didn't dally. "I'm not leaving. Ever."

"Good. Mommy said to come and get you. I bet Grandma and Grandpa will be happy to see you when they get here."

What? My head began to spin.

"Uncle Theo?" he asked when I didn't respond.

"Huh?"

"Are you all right?"

I hoped my forced smile was convincing, since I was cringing internally. "I'm good. Go find Allie and let her know I'll be there in a bit. And tell your dad to come see me while you're at it. I need to talk to him."

By the time I jumped out of the shower and returned to my room, Paxton was sitting at the foot of my bed.

"A little warning would have been nice, P," I grumbled, sporting my boxers, running my towel over my short hair.

His hands came up in a peacekeeping manner. "I'm sorry, but Alissa told me that our weekend brunch was brought up to today since Mom and Dad aren't around tomorrow."

"So I have her to blame for this?" I snorted. "Do they know yet?" Paxton shook his head indicating the negative. "You know this has disaster written all over it, right?"

"T…" Paxton sighed.

"I'm just worried. You know how Mom gets. And then there's Dad…" I rummaged through my rucksack for a t-shirt and slid it over my head when I found one.

"That's all in the past," Paxton said, getting to his feet. "If there's one thing I can tell you about our old man is that losing you has changed him. You know…after we got the news about you, he told me that his biggest regret was not being able to tell you that he was proud of you."

"In case you forgot, he had some pretty nasty things to say that last day right before I left, P."

There was pain in his eyes as he set his lips in a thin line "Face it, what you did was stupid, and if memory serves, your words weren't so eloquent either." Making for the hallway, he paused by the door. "They'll be here in about half an hour. If, God forbid, this turns out to be a complete clusterfuck, I've got your six, bro."

"Thanks, man." Before he closed the door behind him, I smirked. "By the way, nice shiner."

The man laughed. "Glad to see your jaw hasn't kept you

from boasting, G.I. Joe. I'm sure Mom will have something to say when she sees we were up to our old antics."

As long as someone thought to hide the wooden spoons, we'd all be safe. The tiny woman was hell on wheels when it came to disciplining her sons and we were never too old to suffer the wrath of a spoon beating if the occasion called for it. The memories of her numerous attempts had my smile widening. Maybe being home wasn't going to be so bad after all. I just had to get through today first to see if my assessment would hold up.

Half an hour later, I was alone in the kitchen nursing my cup of coffee when the doorbell rang.

The sound of everyone's laughter, the playful banter between Paxton and my father, and the squeals of excitement my mother made as she fawned over the niece I still had yet to meet and my nephew had me smiling, despite my apprehension. I wanted to be a part of what was going on. I had missed too much already.

It's now or never. Setting my mug on the counter, I put one hesitant foot in front of the other and moved toward the living room.

My parents' backs were to me when I entered. Paxton straightened his stance, as he looked my way. "Mom. Dad. I–" His eyes stayed on me.

"Paxton, what–" My mother turned around to see what her youngest son was looking at. Her hand flew to her mouth on a gasp while the other reached blindly toward Dad, clutching his shirt.

"Hilda, what's the…" The man's voice faltered as he turned to see what had gotten his wife in a fit, his face losing its blood. "It can't be."

"T-theo?" Mom whispered. "But–"

"We buried you," Dad supplied.

Let me explain. When the chaplain delivered the news of my death to my family, everyone had been told that I'd perished with the rest of my unit when my Humvee was found in a smoldering pile of rubble. The only thing left had been my dog tags.

"Is it really you?" My mother looked at me as if I were a feat of magic about to disappear before her very eyes.

I took a few steps toward them, unable to control the wetness that began to ease itself down my cheeks. My parents sported mirroring teary gazes. "Mama, it's me. I swear."

The woman hiccupped, her knees giving way as Dad helped ease her down into the chair behind her. Paxton tended to her while Dad took the necessary steps, grabbed my shoulders and looked at me from top to bottom before crushing me in his embrace. Arms trapped at my sides, I stiffened, not quite sure what to make of it. My brother was right. This wasn't the man I remembered.

"God damn, I thought I'd lost you," he said on a broken sob.

Never in my life have I ever seen my father like this. In my arms, the man shook as if the years had made him soft. Frail, even. This was new, and unsettling, to say the least.

"I'm sorry, Dad," I croaked, my arms winding around him, holding his shaking body in case he collapsed. "I'm so sorry I couldn't come back or send someone to let you guys know that I was safe."

Dad's voice cracked when he said, "We'll deal with that later, son." His hands grabbed hold of the sides of my face, giving it a subtle but abrupt shake. It's as if he couldn't bear to let me go just yet. Releasing me, he wiped the back of his hand across his eyes and looked over at Mom. "Your mother needs you."

Mom was in shock, a shaking shell of herself. She was mumbling…her words indecipherable, her head shaking from left to right in disbelief. It wasn't until I crouched down so she could see my face that her rambling stopped. Her eyes met and held mine as her hands reached up and clasped both of my cheeks. "Theo?"

"It's me, Mama." My lips quivered as I tried to smile for her. "I'm back and I'm never leaving again."

I never expected what came next. "I'd have two minds to whoop your ass right now, boy! Don't you ever scare me like that again, do you hear!" I couldn't help the boisterous laugh that escaped me. Yes, my tiny spitfire of a mother still had it in her. Smacking me in the arm, her humored gaze softened. "I thought a part of me died the day they came and…" Not finishing, she threw herself into my arms, knocking me to the floor onto my ass and sobbing into my chest as I cradled her on my lap until she calmed.

"My baby's back," she repeated over and over, peppering my face with kisses, her arms holding on for dear life. Much to my surprise, I felt my father kneeling in behind me, surrounding me in a parent sandwich. "He's back, honey," Mom whispered. "He's really back."

"I know, sweetheart."

Mom sniffled. "Thank God for second chances!"

The bittersweet mood was broken when Jasper interrupted our moment. "Daddy, I'm hungry."

Within seconds, Dad snorted a small laugh, Mom giggled, and when I looked up, my brother was shaking his head, a grin on his face as he looked at his son, holding his wife against his side. Allie's giggle was mixed with sniffles as she held Abigail close with one arm, a hand wiping away the tears she'd shed.

Retiring to the patio while Alissa put the kids to bed for the night, Paxton handed me a beer before asking, "So what're you going to do now that you're back?"

"I don't know." I sighed. This reintegration thing was a hell of a lot more daunting than I'd anticipated. "I was thinking about following through with what I wanted to do after college. Go into construction."

"Seriously?" I nodded. "I would have thought that you'd settle with something more glamorous than that, what with that engineering degree of yours and all."

"I prefer to work with my hands, P. Always have." And I wasn't sure if I could deal with the corporate aspect of things that came with working for a firm. I liked the idea of being my own boss. It offered me the sense of control I found I always needed since my capture. I couldn't be anyone's puppet right now. Maybe not ever.

"So you're really not going back?" I saw the worry in his face.

"I received my honorable discharge before I left that hellhole." Uncle Sam's had me at their beck and call long enough. "With everything that happened on my last mission, I'd be of no use to them now. Plus, my head's too fucked up to keep up with their games. So no…I'm not going back."

"I sense that there's more to what you're telling me," Paxton swallowed before continuing, "but I have a feeling that you don't care to share, nor do I really want you to re-live it either."

"Not particularly. I'll give you more details some time, but I just can't right now, brother. Not after seeing what you've all been through. I wish I'd never gone along with my CO's orders."

"Doesn't sound like you had much choice in the matter."

That was true. My superiors had included me in their plan and set the ball in motion long before I'd even entered the picture. "I didn't."

"So did these super spy operations, as Jasper calls them, work out at least?"

I groaned and looked toward the horizon. "Some of it. Sure as shit wasn't any James Bond-double-oh-seven kind of shit, that's for sure."

My brother laughed without much humor. "Can't say I'm surprised Hollywood's got it all wrong. The guy jumps out of a plane and his suit still keeps its pleats."

I groaned at the visual. There'd been no suits. Hell, some-times there'd been no food or anything beyond a few drops of clean water to drink, and you know you've had it good when you start missing the outhouses you once detested to take a dump in at base camp. Keeping with the subject, I steered things away from me. "Since we're talking about work…" My gaze made its way to my brother. "I read your book."

Paxton's head never snapped so damn fast in my direction before. His reaction was comical. "You did?"

Chuckling, I said, "Yeah." His eyes grew soft, despite his cocky smirk. "It was some really great work, P. Thinking of writing another?"

"Thanks. Maybe…I've been working on something new."

"Well, if you decide to have that one published, know that I'll be the first to read it." I grinned. "Seeing as we're on the topic of you, little brother, how the hell did you land Allie? The woman seems to be too much of a saint to be with someone like you."

"Don't let the halo fool you." I turned at my sister-in-law's words. The woman sported a grin, her eyes twinkling as she eyed my brother. "It's fully tarnished, and my devil's pitchfork is retractable."

Paxton laughed and pulled her so she sat on his lap, depositing a kiss where her neck met her shoulder.

I laughed. "It would explain that stunt in the pub last night. I never thought that my little brother, of all people, would be the one coming out of a restroom with a partner—and be the one blushing."

"I have that effect on him every now and again." She winked at him.

Lifting my beer to the woman, I said, "I like you more and more, Allie," and downed the last of it. "Well, at the risk of looking like an old man, I'm still jet-lagged and, frankly, I have a long day of figuring out how to live a normal life again come tomorrow morning. I'm calling it a night."

"Goodnight," Paxton said along with his wife.

I patted him on the back and then leaned over to kiss the top of Allie's head. "Goodnight, sis. P."

CHAPTER 4

Two weeks, some advertising, and loads of paperwork later, TL Construction & Engineering was born and open for business.

Thanks to Jake Landen and his expert advice on small businesses—Paxton's best buddy helped me with a few legal hurdles for a nominal fee.

Before I could start thinking about tools and equipment, I knew I needed a reliable vehicle, not to mention another method to load up the larger pieces of machinery I'd be needing, depending on the jobs I'll be working. My new Ford Super Duty truck definitely fit the bill, along with the closed-in trailer that now boasted my company logo on its sides and rear. Things were definitely taking shape at a whirlwind pace.

Shopping for a home for myself had been next on my to-do list, and had proven to be easier than I had expected.

I stumbled upon an old Victorian farmhouse on the outskirts of the city. It was dilapidated and in desperate need of some tender love and care, but it had always been the kind of house I wanted. So I jumped on the opportunity, despite being told by the realtor that I'd be best levelling the place and building something new on its land. The place was a major gut, that was true, but it was bound to be a place of pride when I was done with it.

Less than a week after TL was established, calls began to pour in. It left me wondering how in the hell I would find the time to turn my new digs from the deathtrap it was to the vision I held in my mind. But business was business, and money was going to be needed to effect the required changes. I'd just have to deal with spending all of my extra time tending to my own house. Then again, I wasn't much into the social scene like I once was.

Over the course of the next week, I played Mr. Fix-It for a lady whose husband had botched what was, in my opinion, a simple basement renovation. I'd ended up having to run new electrical, as well as fix plumbing, not to mention some structural issues, and wait for the lot to be inspected and approved. All this before getting to what the initial project was all about, the esthetics. Come Friday night, and after the long and frustrating hours I'd pulled, I was relieved to have a moment to myself beyond an hour.

Imagine my surprise when my phone rang with an unknown number that same night.

"Is this TL Construction?" a panicked female voice sounded over the receiver as soon as I answered.

"It is. Can I help you?"

"I hope so. You're the only one I've called who's picked up."

Probably because it's eight o'clock on a Friday night, lady, I thought, but told her, "Listen, not to be rude or anything, but it's after hours, so why don't you tell me what it is exactly that you're calling about?" I grabbed for the bottle of *Bud Light* I had been nursing for the last hour while I was stripping away some drywall in the kitchen and tilted it back.

"I need someone to come and plug up my hole?"

Sputtering, I choked out an, "Excuse me?"

"My kitchen roof is leaking. The water's run into my living room and converted it to an indoor pool, and–"

"Ah!"

Her sigh was heavy with exhaustion. "I know it's late, and on a Friday no less, but is there any chance I can persuade you into checking things out? I'll pay extra, if that's what it takes."

"What's your address?" I found myself asking, disbelieving the fact that I was about to let my home project go down the proverbial poop shoot when I hadn't had the time all week to work on it.

After acquiring her details and hanging up, I loaded my toolbox in the back of the truck, along with anything else necessary for a leaking roof, and jumped in. I may have been pulled away from my own work, but I wasn't going very far. I suppose that was a plus.

About a mile down from my home, a rather pitiful sign boasting Lilianna's Buds greets me. It seems that the field of sunflowers I'd been staring at over my morning coffee for the last week belonged to her. I turned into the crushed rock driveway, parking alongside a beat up black Dodge Caravan with a matching decal to the sign at the property's entrance.

The moment I exited my truck, the sweet fragrance of flowers assaulted me. Something told me that if I happened into her old dilapidated barn, hers wouldn't carry the smell of horseshit like mine did. Or maybe it did, what with the two newer greenhouse-looking structures behind said barn.

I stood by my truck, sussing out the place. I spotted the most likely problematic section of the house almost immediately. From the outside, this house wasn't much better than mine. The addition was fairly recent, and didn't quite match the era or the style of the home. Whoever had built it hadn't done the place justice. Much like the house and barn, the garage was in desperate need of a facelift too.

I walked up the stone steps and knocked on the solid oak door. Sporting a grin, I blurted the first thing that came to mind when the door opened. I also wished I had had a bit more tact as soon as, "I'm here to plug up your hole," had spilled out.

The woman's eyebrows arched upward as her eyes appraised my appearance. "Do you always shoot sexual innuendos to your female clients?"

Heat climbed my face. "No, ma'am. I'm sorry if it came off that way." Apparently ten years spent in the desert and infrequent downtime left a silver-tongued man with a severe case of foot-in-mouth disease. Quick on the recovery, I stuck out my hand. "I'm Theo Lowell from TL Construction."

She blinked a few times, but didn't accept my hand. Huffing, she said, "I don't know what to do. I've got buckets and pots everywhere, but it's getting worse, and I can't seem to stay on top of…"

Her words faded away as I took in my latest client's dishevelled appearance. She was drenched right through her clothes. Her already skin-tight tank top was plastered to her upper body and her shorts stuck to her hips and thighs. The outfit did nothing to conceal and everything to accentuate her assets, right down to her tiny little pink-toed feet. Her wet blond hair hung limp over her breasts and whatever makeup she might have been wearing was all but washed away, or perhaps she didn't wear much, judging by the clear beads of water cascading down her cheeks. She was the epitome of what a country girl looked like in my mind. Natural was my kind of sexy.

A very virile piece of my anatomy had taken notice of this, making this first meeting feel even more awkward. I shifted my stance trying to count down from one hundred, hoping she wouldn't notice my body's reaction. She'd most likely kick me out and report my ass as some kind of creeper.

"Mr. Lowell?"

"Huh?" She was staring as if waiting for me to say something. "Oh, right. Can I come in and take a look?"

"Please. It's in the kitchen."

The minute I walked into the aforementioned room, I knew that my assumption had been right.

"Looks like it could be the joint from the addition to the

existing structure," I hypothesised aloud. "I'll need to get up on the roof, ma'am. Let me go get my ladder."

"It's Morgan."

"What?"

"Please don't call me ma'am." Her smile was coy. "That's a title for women my mother's age. And you won't need a ladder."

"If I want to take a look at your roof—"

She shook her head. "Trust me, you don't need a ladder. You can get to it from my bedroom." She walked past me. "Follow me."

Taking a look had entailed a little more work than I would have liked. Since the kitchen's roof had been used as a balcony off of the master bedroom, I ended up removing slats of decking before I could assess the problem. Great idea, bad execution, though. When I finally got to the root of the problem, I groaned. Morgan wasn't going to like what I had to say.

As I came back in from the torrential downpour that had yet to let up, she asked, "So?" and handed me a towel so I could mop myself up a bit.

"I hope you have insurance." I dabbed at my face, running the towel through my hair.

"I do, but what's the matter?"

"The damage is far more extensive than I thought it would be. To be honest, I'm surprised you haven't had a leak until now. You're lucky your roof hasn't come down on top of your head."

Horror spread across her features. "It's that bad?" I nodded. She turned and began to pace the room and muttered, "I could kill you, Steve!" under her breath.

"Pardon?"

"Nothing," she was quick to say.

Who was Steve? Where was the man? And more importantly, why the hell was I interested in those details?

It wasn't until Morgan led me out of her bedroom, the one with the balcony, that I spotted the frame on the bedside table and did a double take. There, behind the glass, was a photo of Damon with his arms wrapped around her, both of them sporting goofy grins at what looked like some kind of social gathering judging, by the beer in his hand.

My feet stopped moving as memories of *that* day hit me like a ton of bricks. The explosion. Damon slouching dead in the driver's seat of our Humvee. My capture. Suddenly, Morgan's bedroom started feeling like a shrinking box and I could feel my extremities going numb while my breath came out in short pants.

Shortly after Morgan had left the room, she returned when she realized I hadn't followed. "What is it?" she asked, which made me look over at her and then back to the photo. Her gaze followed mine. "Did you know Steve?"

Steve? No, that's Damon. Clearing my throat, I said, "He looks familiar," since the names didn't match. *Maybe it's not him.* But my relief was short-lived with Morgan's next words.

"Oh! I keep forgetting." She palmed her forehead. "He preferred his middle name to his first. Especially in the service. He went by Damon."

"Smyth?" My voice quivered.

At her nod, my heart sunk and my head began to whirl. The heavy weight on my chest that had caused me to pant earlier was back.

Morgan's gaze zeroed in on me. "Did you know him?"

Words evaded me. *Sorry for your loss* just didn't seem to cut it in my opinion so I choked out an, "I knew him. He was a great man, a great friend." The woman nodded, and I kept rambling like a bumbling idiot, but I couldn't let on as to how close he and I had become during our deployment. I couldn't tell her that he'd been in my unit, that I'd seen firsthand what had happened to him. "This is why I never married. I couldn't leave a wife behind if something ever happened to me while I was over there. I–"

"Hold on, wife?" Her voice was high-pitched. Then the woman in front of me burst out laughing.

While Morgan was busy giggling herself silly, my mind took me back to when I'd first met Damon. He'd only ever talked about three women in his life. Morgan had been mentioned a time or two, but I believe Kayla, I think it was, was his wife's name. At the time of his death, they'd had a beautiful two-year-old daughter, Savannah, whom he'd shown me numerous pictures of. They'd been the loves of his life. And he'd left a sister behind. One I was now face-to-face with.

On one last chuckle, Morgan broke me from my thoughts. "I was engaged once, but not to that idiot. Steve, aka Damon is...*was* my brother." I could only nod at what I'd figured out on my own. The question about where her man was still burned at me, but my curiosity was put to rest just as quickly as the inquiry had manifested itself. "As for my fiancé," her tone was pure ice, "he's been gone for about as long as my brother has been."

"I'm sorry, Morgan." She had no idea how sorry I was.

She shrugged. "I'm not. He wasn't a good man. He–" Her mouth snapped shut, her cheeks pinked. "I don't know why I just told you that."

"It's fine."

"Can we get back to business?"

Gladly! "Let me get a few things and I'll see what I can do to hold off the water for the night. We'll need to wait for things to dry up a bit before I can do anything permanent outside, though." On that note, and without waiting for a response from her, I made my escape for the front door.

CHAPTER 5

Thankful for the thick tarp I had in the back of my truck, I covered Morgan's roof and sealed the points of entry I found. She'd also have to let me know how and when she wanted me to proceed with the repairs.

"So that's just temporary right?" she asked when I came back in.

I nodded. "The addition wasn't done right. I'm not sure if you want to keep that patio up there but if so…"

She huffed her frustration as we headed down to the main floor. "Can I ask you something?" Bending over to grab a pot that was on the verge of overflowing, she proceeded to the kitchen sink and emptied it before setting it back in place.

I took the time to appreciate the view of those short shorts that were suctioned and riding up her perfectly rounded ass. "Sure."

"I've been working on this place for what seems nonstop." She ran a shaky hand over her forehead and into her hair, gathering it up into a messy bun on the top of her head. I could tell the woman was stressed. "I can't seem to stay on top of things, and with running my business and this issue popping up, the fact that you have to most likely gut my kitchen to fix it…You are going to fix it, right?"

"If that's what you want, of course."

"Well I can't very well have a gaping hole in my kitchen ceiling, can I?" she snapped. Covering her face while shaking her head from side to side, she took a cleansing breath. "I'm sorry. It's just…I can't do this alone. I need someone to help me rebuild this place from top to bottom, like I've envisioned."

"You could sell it and save yourself a lot of hassle," I suggested.

"No." Her expression was solemn. "This is the last place…"

Not only did I regret my question, but I despised myself for putting that sad look on her face. "No need to explain. I got it."

"I just don't know where to start anymore. This was supposed to be a family project of sorts. Me and Steve…I mean, Damon and Kayla, his wife. We were supposed to take this place and turn it around. But now, every time I get started on a project, something else happens that needs to be replaced or fixed right away. I…" Her voice trailed off on an emotionally charged sigh.

"I'm not going to lie to you, Morgan, this isn't a small job. I can see about hiring a reliable crew to work around here–"

"No!"

No?

"I want to learn to do it on my own." She bit her lip. The innocent act sent a zing straight to my dick. "It's something I need to do. For myself."

"I'm confused. You said you needed help, but you want to do it on your own? What am I missing here?"

She gazed down at her feet. "I want you to teach me." It came out as a whisper. When she looked back up, I could see a blush begin to fade. "I swear I won't get in the way. I just want to be able to say that I've done something from start to finish for once in my life. To prove…" She never finished her sentence, but I somehow understood where she was headed with that last statement, and I couldn't help but feel for the tiny woman. Someone had been disappointed in her at some point and she was looking to prove them wrong.

"Okay." I can't believe I'd said it. There were so many reasons why I should have said the opposite, but I hadn't, and now I was obliged to her. I chalked my latest bout of temporary insanity to the chill from the rainwater. It must have turned my brain into a block of ice.

She seemed as shocked at my answer as I was. "Okay?"

"Yeah, okay," I said, and hoped I wouldn't regret my decision, even though I could see red flags flashing in my mind. "First thing's first. You need to call your insurance."

"Already done. They'll be here first thing tomorrow morning."

"Good. Next, I'll need you to compile a list of things you're looking to have done here. I want to know everything from plumbing and electrical to the simplest of paint jobs." To be honest, with what I'd seen of her place so far, I thought every square inch of her place needed help.

"Sure. I can take you through the rest of the house now, if you'd like." She bit that lower lip of hers again.

Dear God, give me strength! I wasn't quite sure what I was asking for strength for, but I had a list that was becoming a mile long with all the reasons I should find her a new contractor. But I wouldn't. Call me crazy, but as much as my tie to her brother should be keeping me away from her in all aspects, my overwhelming feeling of guilt made me feel like I owed him. I felt responsible because had he been here, he would have helped her.

A couple of hours later, I walked out of Morgan's house with a long list of things she wanted to tackle, as well as a longer list of things I noticed that needed immediate attention, not to mention some photos and measurements of all the rooms we would eventually be tackling.

"Give me the weekend to work on some draft drawings of those changes we discussed. I'll get you some quotes for the options, and have it to you first thing Monday," I told her. "You can take the day or however long you want to decide or change things since I have a job to finish up with, but then, if you're ready, I'm all yours."

"Thanks, Mr. Lowell." Her face brightened up, the stress

lines that were present in her features earlier having disappeared.

"If we're going to work together, call me Theo."

"Thanks, Theo."

Exhausted from a long day, adding to it a long and drenched night, I sauntered through the front door of my house and locked up. I pealed my wet clothes off as I climbed the stairs toward the bathroom, jumped into the shower, pipes rattling in the walls and all, then crawled into bed.

CHAPTER 6

When Monday came around, I woke feeling as if some-one had hit me with a Mac truck. My stomach was churning, my muscles ached and my head pounded. It sure as hell didn't help that I hadn't slept much all weekend long. I'd been busy working on those drawings for Morgan.

After dropping said drawings and cost workup with Morgan, I headed over to the Tanners' to finish up with their basement-renovation-gone-awry. By mid-afternoon, I was driving up my neighbor's driveway after she'd called me, requesting that I come over to discuss my work.

The weather had made a turn for the better, but with the sweltering heat of the mid-summer sun and the worsening of my symptoms, I was hoping that I could get home early for some much needed rest.

Over the weekend Morgan's insurance company had sent a crew in to dry up the place with dehumidifiers and fans. An adjuster had also been by to suss out the damages and calculate what kind of compensation she should expect, and what her options were. I was appalled to see that no one had been by to start with the cleaning, so I jumped to work.

I was finishing up with cutting out most of the drywall to her kitchen ceiling when she asked me, "Are you sure you're all right to work?" This had been the fifth time she'd inquired since my arrival. I must have looked as bad as I felt.

Brushing off her comment, I paused to close my eyes and

take a deep breath to stave off my rather constant nausea before I climbed down the stepladder.

"I'm fine. So, what did you think about the drawings?"

"They look gorgeous, but…" She snagged her bottom lip between her teeth. I knew I was really under the weather when her action barely registered with my body.

"With what you're looking at right now, it's not that much more," I said, knowing that she was worried about the end dollar amount. All clients were, since it didn't take much to throw a project over budget. "The insurance is covering the entire kitchen, with the exception of the flooring, right?" She nodded. "Anything else?"

"They'll cover the kitchen floor if one of those tiles cracks, since I don't have any extra tiles to replace them with, but I want it changed anyway. If the top of this room isn't done right, I'm not sure I can trust the bottom." I nodded in understanding. "They're replacing the carpet, baseboards and painting for the entire first floor since the water spread everywhere."

"You said you wanted to make this place look like the addition matches the original rest of the house. The only way to do that is to expand the upstairs."

"Yes, I get that. It's just…" Her brows furrowed. "Can we actually get that done with just you and me? I mean, when my brother and I added the kitchen we had six other guys working every day for a month to get it done. What you're showing me here is practically an entire demolition of nearly the entire upstairs half of my house. How am I supposed to live here if my entire house is being done at once? I can't–"

"I'm trying to give you what you want." I met her eyes. After all, she's the one who'd asked for those drawings. "You said you wanted authenticity and this," I pointed to my weekend's work, "would alleviate any future complications, such as the one you're stuck with now. Add the extra square footage and the resale value on this place would be through the roof. Just think about the gigantic walk-in closet you'll get along with an enlarged en suite."

Her eyes narrowed. "Excuse me?"

I should have stopped there but I kept on rambling, Morgan crossing her arms over her bloused chest. "Most women would be chomping at the bit for that kind of closet space. Just think of–"

"I'm not most women." The woman tapped her heeled foot. What the hell was she doing in that corporate looking skirted suit anyway?

"What? Am I wrong, Miss Smyth?"

"It's Morgan. The least you could do is give me the same curtesy I give you by using your name, *Mr. Lowell.*" She took the couple of steps she needed to face off with me. "And while we're at it, I'm not going to let you bully me into spending a fortune just to get my house up to *your* liking. Do what I hired you to do."

I snorted. "You mean plug your hole?"

"For starters, yeah." She opened her mouth to add something, but ended up closing it, a blush spreading over her features.

Holding my hands up, I stepped back a pace. "Hey, your words, not mine."

"And when are you going to show me how to do some of this stuff?" The continuously tapping shoe on the floor was beginning to annoy me.

"How about when you reach a final decision about those drawings," I said, *and change into those tiny shorts and tanks of yours.* "I can tell you're still thinking about them, so how about this…" I coughed into my elbow, but that made the sudden tickle in my throat worse, so I coughed some more.

"I think you should go home."

I shook my head in response, clearing my throat in the crook of my elbow. "I'm fine." But I knew I wasn't. Before I could finish what I had started to say, another coughing fit hit and the room began to spin. Closing my eyes and breathing to regain my balance, I grabbed on to the closest thing to me for assistance. Morgan.

"Theo?"

"Hmm?" Opening my eyes to look at her, I found myself with a handful of breast. Retracting my hand, the view before me began to tilt.

One minute I was standing, feeling embarrassed, the next, my ass made contact with the floor, my legs having gone soft. I swear I heard Morgan's panicked, "Oh my God!" while blood thundered through my ears and my vision went black.

CHAPTER 7

Something cold on the back of my neck and on my forehead made me open my eyes. *Where the hell am I?*

"Theo?"

I found myself staring into light brown eyes that reminded me of melted milk chocolate, swallowing to get past the dryness in my throat. "What happened?"

"I think you need to get home. You're sick," she said. "Can you get up?"

"Yeah." The minute I got to my feet, my sea legs were back, threatening to give way once more. Morgan grabbed hold of me, wrapping one of my arms over her shoulder and hers around my waist. I heard her grunt. "You can't carry me."

"Watch me."

"No, seriously." I struggled to stand up straighter. "I'll snap you like a twig you're so small. I can walk."

"You can't even stand without support, so the way I see it is that you let me be your crutch, and we'll try for the couch," she said with a no-nonsense tone.

"Yes, ma'am!" Despite my feeling like shit, humor laced my words. Her eyes narrowed on me. "Sorry. You reminded me of my mother for a second."

"Great." She blew a puff of air to move the strands of hair that had fallen into her face with no success. "Think you can walk now, smartass? I think you might be right about snapping me in half. You're not that small."

"How about you walk me to my truck and I'll be off? I won't need my tools, so if it's okay with you, I'll leave them here."

She nodded.

With more of an effort from me, we managed to get to the truck, but my head began to whirl again after I got behind the wheel. I rested my forehead on the steering wheel as I tried to regain my bearings, but no amount of breathing seemed to alleviate the dizziness or the dark spots that clouded my peripheral vision. The short walk from the house to the truck had been more exhausting than I wanted to admit.

"Let's get you to the passenger seat, I'm driving you." I didn't argue. After making a right toward town, she asked, "Where to?"

"Make a left at the next driveway."

"But–"

"Are you bringing me home or not?"

"This is your home?" she asked as she took in the sight of the old worn exterior, the weathered barn that was half collapsed onto itself, the grass in drastic need of being trimmed, and the rose bushes that looked more like green barbwire designed to keep the owner confined to their house, where I must admit, might not be as safe for them as the great outdoors.

"This is home."

"We're neighbours?"

"We're neighbours," I repeated.

"Well I guess I don't have to worry about taking a cab home, huh?"

"Guess not," I said weakly with my head leaning against the cool glass of the passenger side window. I groaned at the subtle relief the coolness offered.

"You okay? I can–"

"Go on home."

"Take all the time you need, to get better, I mean." She offered a smile and my keys.

"I'll be as good as new tomorrow."

CHAPTER 8

I wish I could say that I was better the next day, but such wasn't the case. I woke up, barely able to stand without falling down. My sense of balance, compounded with the incessant nausea and the fact that I could barely hold anything down, made me crawl back under the sheets and fall into another one of my dream cycles.

I was woken up by a hand shaking me, my throat feeling hoarse, but not from the endless bouts of coughing. It was one I had grown quite accustomed to over the years since my deployment. The one caused by screaming.

"Wake up, baby," I heard.

Mom! "Mom?" I tried to sit up, but the bout of nausea made me roll onto the opposite side of the mattress and reach for the large bowl I had brought up with me in case I couldn't make it to the bathroom.

When I managed to curb the urge to upchuck, I lay back down, closing my eyes against the daylight coming through my bedroom window and breathing things out. I really needed to get some blinds installed.

The back of my mother's hand landed on my forehead. "You're running a fever, sweetie. How long have you felt like this?"

"Since yesterday," I croaked. "How'd you know I was home?"

"Your truck's in the driveway and your father jimmied the lock on the door when we heard you screaming." She had tears in her eyes. "Theo, what–"

"It's nothing. I'm fine."

She nodded, but the look in her eyes told me that I'd failed at convincing her.

After refusing to let her bring me home with her and my father, dad left her in charge while he went out to run a few errands. Mom made soup and tended to me, despite her non-stop cursing of the firetrap—as she called it—I had chosen to buy and live in.

By late afternoon, I felt well enough to get myself down-stairs to the couch for a change of scenery. No longer as ex-hausted as I was, I figured the living room—or what I had of one—was a good place to veg. The TV sat on a bunch of large boxes and I'd managed to have the cable installed late last week, so I was good to go.

"Are you sure you don't need me to stay?" Mom asked when my father had arrived to pick her up.

"I'll be fine, Mama."

"All right. I'll call later to check up on you." She kissed my forehead. "If you need anything at all, call us."

"Will do. Thanks for helping."

"You know I wouldn't have it any other way, baby boy." Her endearment made me smile.

The woman left and was replaced with another. One I hadn't expected.

"You're not dead," she said. "I guess that's good."

"Shit, Morgan!" All I was sporting were my boxers and a t-shirt. Reaching for the throw from the back of the couch, I covered myself as fast as I could. "What are you doing here?"

"I figured that my contractor didn't show up today, so I'd best check up on him." Her eyes made a run from my feet up to my face. She gave her head an abrupt shake and smiled shyly. "Was that your mom?"

I nodded. "What's that?" I gestured toward the container in her hands.

"Oh!" She looked down at the item. "I figured that you were still sick and that's why you never bothered to call in, so I made you some soup."

She made soup? "Why?"

She shrugged her shoulders. "I guess I felt bad about what happened yesterday. I-I was worried. Then there's the fact that you're my neighbour and all," she rambled on. "It's sweet and sour soup. My mother used to make it for us when we were kids. It's so much better than chicken noodle."

Her opinion mirrored mine, making me smile. "I know. Mom is set on the old staple, though."

"Of course." She smiled in agreement.

Seconds trickled by, making things feel more awkward. I wasn't sure if it was because I lacked hosting skills, if it was just that she was a client, or what, exactly, but she broke the silence first.

"So is the kitchen okay?" She lifted the soup container. "I should get going and let you rest."

I nodded. "Sure."

I heard her make her way back and head toward the front door without a second glance.

"Morgan?" She turned to look at me with her hand on the doorknob. "Thank you." After a curt nod, she turned and let herself out.

CHAPTER 9

It took me an extra day to get back to feeling right again, but by then Morgan had made her decision. She was going ahead with the top floor addition.

It was Wednesday morning, and Morgan allowed me access to her home dressed in another one of those power suits.

"I'm sorry to do this to you, but I got a call late last night for an emergency meeting with one of my clients," she announced.

"But aren't the insurance contractors coming in to gut the kitchen?"

"That and the flooring." She bit that bottom lip of hers again. "You think you can handle letting them in? I know this isn't optimal, but I really have to handle this. They're one of my largest clients."

"No, that's fine. Did you make sure to tell the insurance company that we were keeping the cabinetry?"

"Yeah. She emailed me the work order for the contractor this morning. I double-checked and it's all in there in the notes. I left a copy for you and the other guy on the kitchen countertop." She smirked. "I figured that he wouldn't miss it if I left it in there."

"Good thinking."

Let's just say that I was glad that I'd been around when those guys showed up. It's a damn good thing that Morgan had handled the packing of the contents of her kitchen cabinets with the way they'd come tearing through her place.

Instead of doing what I should have been doing, which was working on stripping the top of Morgan's kitchen roof in preparation to adding on to the upstairs, I played foreman to the insurance crew.

By the time I caught them taking the first cabinet, the doors cleanly ripped off their hinges, out to the dumpster, I was about to lose my shit.

It had been my recommendation that Morgan keep and reuse the kitchen cabinetry, a recommendation to which she'd agreed. She'd worried at first about the wood warping or having issues with mold, but I assured her that if they were dried and stored properly, they'd be fine. Hell, I even told her that I'd refinish them, change their color if she didn't like the original blond oak coloring. Let's face it, insurance payouts don't cover the replacement of wooden cabinets to the full extent, and since Morgan shuddered at the thought of pressed laminate, it was cost effective on both fronts.

As I finished tearing the lead of the demolition group a new ass hole, a car door slammed behind me. My eyes widened when I saw Morgan heading toward us.

Morgan stomped up her front steps to the two of us. "What's going on here?" she asked. It wasn't until she'd touched my arm that I realized that the foreman and I were standing toe-to-toe. "Theo..." And then came the gasp. "What the hell did you do to my cabinet?" She pointed toward the item in question that sat beside us by the front door.

"We're awfully sorry, ma'am," the man said, a sheepish look on his face, hand rubbing the back of his neck.

I backed away and allowed Miss Smyth to simply jump on in and lay it on thicker than thick on the man.

I hadn't paid much attention to the exchange, a little overly enthralled with the tiny sprite that was taking on a man who was double her size. The kicker was that he actually looked terrified.

Damn she's hot when she's spitting nails.

I took in her posture. She might not have been more than five-five in height to my six feet—in her three inch heels, no less—but her shoulders were held square, chin jutted out stubbornly, and her finger poked him in the chest as she went on and on about the lack of respect and consideration to clientele wishes. I could have very well stood there, watching her all day with that sassy I-know-what-I-want behavior of hers. It made my blood heat and my imagination run away with me as I wondered if she was this passionate about everything in her life. I was willing to bet that she'd look just as appealing, if not better, in the throes of passion. I knew I shouldn't have been thinking about Morgan in that way, but I couldn't help it. Nor did those thoughts last for very long, anyway.

Next thing I knew, Morgan and I are in the entrance to her home as vehicle doors slammed, trucks are started, revved, and are peeling out of the drive.

A loud grumbling knocked me out of my reverie before a loud, "Fuck!" followed closely by the slamming of her front door.

My eyes snapped to Morgan. The woman was wild with fury, that much was certain. How much time had I zoned out for?

"Can this day possibly get any worse?"

I held my tongue at her rhetorical question, watching as she headed toward the kitchen, her heels clacking against the subflooring.

Death wish or not, I followed her. "Morgan?"

"Oh. My. God."

"Morgan?"

She whirled around. "How am I supposed to be able to do anything now? My kitchen is a disaster, and my contractors are gone!"

"It's just for tonight. They'll…"

She bowed her head and I knew that look. Defeat. I'd

worn that one far too many times in my life not to recognize it.

Her voice croaked. "Didn't you hear me out there?" She sniffled. I hate it when women cry. It makes me feel so helpless. "I fired them."

"You what?"

"I need to call my insurance and report this. I'll just take the payout and find someone on my own. The company told me that these guys specialised in restorative measures. That's why I'd agreed to them. So much for that, huh?"

I snorted my agreement. "Calm down. I'm sure they have a list of other contractors you can choose from."

"I don't want any more contractors," she whined. "I just want this mess solved."

Kind of hard to do that without a contractor don't you think, sweetheart?

Molten chocolate eyes aimed daggers my way, proof that I had spoken aloud. "Funny." She gave a deep sigh. "What do you think?"

"Of what?"

"You think you can handle more than just the expansion on this place?" she asked.

"I could."

"I'll be around to help." Her smile was forced, but at least her stress seemed to have leveled off a bit.

"Don't you have a job?" As soon as I said the words, I wanted to take them back when I noticed her eyes shimmering again.

"Umm…" It wasn't a yes, but it wasn't a no. My guess was that this morning's meeting didn't go according to plan.

"Then what's with–" I waved my hand gesturing up and down at her body, regarding her pencil skirt, the matching blazer, the silk blouse, stockings, and heels.

"I told you, a client meeting. Well, I guess you can call them my ex-client now." She clapped her hands and smirked as she rubbed them together. "Let me go change and I'm all yours…or at least until I can reclaim my kitchen to get back to business."

Fuck! What have I gotten myself into?

Little did I know that last thought was going to be my mantra for the foreseeable future.

CHAPTER 10

It was apparent from the start that I'd bitten off more than I could chew. A week into this construction gig at Morgan's and I was already running behind schedule. Having to teach her about the simplest of tasks was wearing me thin. To recoup some of my lost time, I'd put her on clean-up duty. She didn't say anything about it. If anything, she seemed a little off when I'd arrived this morning; sad, if I was being honest.

Maybe, when she's done, you can send her up to her room to handle the demo that needs to be taken care of? That wasn't a bad idea. The installation of the trusts, the roofing, shingles, and windows was scheduled for this Friday, and part of that happening meant that the master bedroom would need to be packed away, shielded from debris, and the drywall on two of her walls would need to be removed. The room that she was using as an office would need the same treatment as well.

Morgan's body cast a shadow on my work area. "How's it coming along?"

I grunted. Rerouting a water line can sometimes be a bitch, and this time it sure as hell was trying my patience. Add to that Morgan's flowery scent, barely-there cut-off jeans, and thin tank tops, and let's just say that my unrequited attraction to the woman was also part of what had me on edge. "Pass me the pipe wrench, please?" I held my hand out and waited. When the damn thing never came, I turned to look at her expectantly.

"I'm not sure what I'm looking for," she said.

"It's by your right foot." I pointed to it.

Bending over to pick it up, she proceeded to inspect the thing. "This?"

"Will you hand it over, please?" I gritted my teeth.

She popped it into my hand. "You don't have to be so pissy."

My laugh held all the exasperation I felt as I turned back to my work. "Says the girl with no basic tool knowledge."

"What's your problem?"

"My problem?" Finishing up with the wrench, I put it down, then turned to find her, hands on her hips, sporting an irritated expression.

"Yeah, what's your problem? You haven't taught me anything today, you stuck me on cleaning duty, and you're behaving like a jackass!"

I ran a palm down my face in frustration. "I can't work like this. We have two days to get that master prepped for Friday and all you care about is your kitchen. We're behind schedule, Morgan, and since you never bothered to tell me that you knew nothing about anything–"

"I know how to paint!"

I guffawed. "Do you see a fucking wall that's ready for that yet? For Christ's sake, woman, you don't even know the difference between a Reed & Prince and a Phillips screwdriver!"

"I fail to see where this has anything to do with you teaching–"

"I don't have time!" She jumped, her eyes widening at my yelling. Regretting my loss of temper, I decided to shut up and get back to work before I said or did anything I'd regret. Asking her to hire on some temporary help could wait until I'd calmed down.

W hen I finished with the water line, I realized that my habitual flower-scented shadow was absent, and that loud rock music was coming from upstairs.

As I walked up each tread, I became aware of loud banging that accompanied the muffled tune of AC/DC. The closer I got, the words to *Highway to Hell* made my lips quirk up, and then I heard a crash of broken glass.

My steps halted at the only closed door—the door to Morgan's bedroom. I reached for the knob.

The disaster I took in was nothing compared to what I found collapsed in the middle of the floor. By the outside wall lay a sledgehammer and what were remnants of the drywall that used to be her bedroom wall. Morgan had torn down an entire wall and had obviously started on the next, seeing as the large gaping hole was hard to miss.

The next thing that caught my eye was the broken frame that lay on the floor with shards of glass around it. A large one in particular had a substantial amount of blood smeared on its surface.

My feet moved quickly. "Fucking hell, Morgan!" I grabbed the hand that she held pressure to. "Let me see."

"Just get out," she said in a hushed tone, keeping her face averted from me. "I'm fine."

"You're not fine. Let me clean you up."

CHAPTER 11

Leading Morgan to the bathroom, I motioned her back toward the toilet. "Sit down."

She did as I requested. "I'm fine."

"Let me. Where's your First Aid kit?"

"Under the sink."

Fetching it, I kneeled between her legs, popped the kit open and began to look through it, making sure I had what I needed.

"Give me your hand." The heated jolt that hit me then nearly knocked me onto my ass. Focusing on her wound, I was relieved to see that the bleeding had slowed. Taking some gauze, along with some rubbing alcohol, I cleaned the gash that crossed the palm of her hand, eliciting a pain-filled hiss from her. Remembering that my mother used to do this with mine and Paxton's numerous cuts and bruises when we were younger, I blew on her wound. Morgan's breath caught, and my gaze moved to meet hers. "You okay?"

"Yeah." She cleared her throat.

Applying some antibacterial ointment to the cut, I covered it with a bandage and taped it in place.

Finished with my small paramedic stint, I set her First Aid kit back where I'd retrieved it. "Stay here for a bit. You're looking a little pale." Getting to my feet, I took the waste basket with me and left the bathroom to pick up the mess of glass shards that had been left on the floor by her bed.

Kneeling, I grabbed the damaged photo frame, studying the two grinning faces staring back.

"Kayla, Damon's wife, took that one of us before Damon deployed." Morgan's words held a hint of darkness. "We were having a party in Damon's honor."

I nodded, my mouth feeling drier than the Sahara Desert. "You were close," I stated more than asked, looking up at her approaching form.

She sniffled, reaching out for the frame I still held. "Yeah. We did everything together," she explained. "When Mom and Dad died, we looked after each other. We found out about this place through their will. It was our grandparents', only we thought Dad had sold it because of his falling out with them."

"I bet you're wishing that he had, huh?"

"No." Her answer was firm. "As much as this house needs help, this is where Damon and I felt most at home while growing up. We sold our parents' house and moved here and started fixing it up with my sister-in-law, but then he had to leave." She took a seat at the foot of her bed, looking down at the photo. Her tears started up again. "Did you know that today's his birthday?"

My chest tightened, my eyes burned, and my knuckles had gone white from clenching my fists. I shook my head solemnly and whispered, "I'm sorry." After breathing it out for a few seconds, I attempted to lift my head. My eyes found her bloodshot orbs and all I saw was pain, grief, and desolation. The walls began to close in around me. "God, I'm so sorry," I croaked and got to my feet as my vision blurred. "I've got to get out of here."

Without another word, I did just that.

I made it as far as to the side of my truck before the constriction in my chest caused me to halt. The internal dam threatened to give way, but with each passing second, bent over, leaning on my knees, I sucked in much-needed air that seemed to help control my turbulent emotions.

Or so I thought.

Running my hands through my lengthening hair, the military style no longer really distinguishable, I clenched my tresses and kicked the tire as my breathing picked up again due to so many fleeting memories of Damon and the rest of my team. And the first tears from what had transpired three years ago began to fall.

And I allowed them, because I could give into the grief. The guilt. The anger. Unlike three years ago.

I didn't acknowledge the crunching of rocks underfoot, nor the presence beside me, until a gentle hand laid itself on my shoulder. That simple touch proved to be too much, and I found myself crumbling to my knees with Morgan trying to keep me on my feet, and failing miserably.

Forced into straddling my lap, she clutched the back of my neck and hugged me to her chest in a death grip, rocking us back and forth in an effort to soothe the sobs that shook my body.

"You're fine," she whispered after a while, and I felt her lips on the top of my head. "You're safe. It's okay. I'm here."

"If you only knew." My voice quivered.

"Shh." She began to rub my back.

Feeling one of her tears trickle down the side of my face, I pulled away, her arms giving a little at her grip. I chanced a look at her, and couldn't help but cup the sides of her face and brush the tears that had streaked her cheeks with the pads of my thumbs.

The look of emotional turmoil. The pain. *You did this to her.* I cast my eyes downward, the guilt and shame overwhelming me. "I shouldn't be here." But I couldn't bring myself to leave.

"Y-you were there." She gulped. "You didn't just know him in passing, did you?"

I shook my head. "He was with my team."

"You know what happened?"

"More than anyone else." I closed my eyes and took a deep breath, the air in my lungs having turned to fire. "I'm the only one left from that day. I relive it every single day, Morgan."

Her breath released with a whoosh. "Sergeant T?" I hadn't heard that moniker in far too many years, which had my eyes snapping to hers. I nodded, her eyes widening.

Instead of plying me with questions, her hands tightened on the sides of my neck and pulled me back in. I knew I shouldn't, but my arms wrapped around her and pulled her tight against me as more sobs broke the surface on both our parts.

As we regained our wits, I buried my face in Morgan's neck. She smelled of flowers and fresh air mixed with a subtle hint of sweat from her labor. It was soothing and intoxicating all at once.

Nuzzling the pulse by her ear, I felt heat flare on the skin beneath my lips. "I'm sorry," I whispered and kissed her where I had just nuzzled and pulled back to hold her face between my palms. "I'm so sorry," I kissed her cheek. "I'm so fucking sorry, Morgan," I said yet again and kissed her other cheek as my body shook with so much pent up remorse that had yet to be released. "I'm—"

Her lips crushed mine in a kiss that seared. I tasted her sweetness combined with the salt of our mixed tears. When her tongue traced the seam of my mouth, I opened for her, and she moaned as velvet met velvet.

Knowing I needed to get control of myself, I slowed things down. We sipped at each other before I finally pulled away and laid my forehead against hers.

Trying to regain my breath, I looked at the woman before me; her face flushed and blotchy from her tears, her eyes closed. The tension that had been present in her expression earlier was absent.

Rubbing my nose against hers, she opened her eyes, and my regret was instantaneous when I saw the fires of passion in them.

"Theo," she whispered at the same time I said, "Morgan."

She leaned in for another go, and as much as it thrilled me that our attraction was mutual, I couldn't allow myself to give in, no matter how much I wanted to. So I turned my head to the side. Morgan pulled back and when our eyes met, all traces of passion had left, and in its stead, hurt reigned. She looked as if I'd slapped her across the face.

"I can't."

"Why not?"

"I just…" I shook my head and sighed. "I can't."

She grabbed my face, forcing my eyes to meet hers. "At least look at me when you're rejecting me. I think I deserve that much."

"You deserve that and a lot more than what I can give you, Morgan. I just can't."

"You've said that already." She shoved my shoulders and got up off of me.

"I'm no good."

"What am I, seventeen?" She huffed, crossing her arms over her chest. "I think I can figure out what's good for me and what's not, Theo. I'm a grown-ass woman."

"I'd say you're right, but in this case…" I allowed my voice to trail off.

She threw her hands up in the air in defeat, "Fine!" then turned on her heel, heading toward the house. "I'll see you tomorrow," she said, slamming the door behind her.

I got to my feet, dusted off my jeans and jumped in the truck, cranking it. "Yeah, tomorrow," I said to no one in particular.

CHAPTER 12

A near sleepless night, a cold shower, and some palm action later, my desire to be near, to hold, to possess Morgan had only grown stronger. The dream I had of her when I managed to fall asleep for all but a few hours had definitely not helped my situation, either.

The mere memory of Morgan's lips on mine, her taste, the way she gave as much as she got had my dick standing at attention in seconds. It's too bad I couldn't be with her. Not after all the heartache I'd caused her. But she didn't know the half of it.

Still, part of me felt like an ass for pushing her away, while the other felt justified that I had done the right thing. She deserved to be happy, to be loved, to feel whole and cherished by a whole man. And I wasn't one of those anymore. I hadn't been for a while. Not since *that* day.

Giving up on sleep, and regardless of the above, I lay awake trying to come up with reasons to justify that I could be the man for her. Fuck, did I ever want to be.

But you can't.

There was nothing aside from my body and physical release that I could offer anyone—especially her. I was nothing but a shell of a man, a broken one at that.

No, I was better off alone. Miserable.

People don't get hurt when you don't get involved with them. It was for the best. Trust me, I know it's a cop-out, but it beats me failing anyone again. I wouldn't be able to live with myself if I failed again.

Running a hand through my hair and down my face, I got

ready for another day at Morgan's, dread mixing with anticipation.

I parked the truck and dragged my feet toward the front steps as Morgan pinned something on the door and practically ploughed into me as she turned to rush toward her van, if the jingling of the keys in her hand were any indication.

"Whoa!" I grabbed onto her upper arms. "Where are you going in a hurry?"

"Theo," she said a little breathlessly. "I…uh," she paused to swallow. "I won't be around for the next couple of days."

She was avoiding me. The realization held a lot more disappointment than warranted.

Yet, weren't you the one who wanted distance? "I thought you said that you didn't have to work?"

"I don't, but something else came up." She avoided my gaze.

"Is everything all right?"

"Sure, why wouldn't it be?"

I shrugged. Because of that kiss. Because I can't get you out of my head. Because you clearly want more than what happened—and maybe so do I. Instead I said, "When will you be back?"

"Monday at the latest. Look, I need to get going." She turned and ripped the paper, which looked like a note, off of the door. "I know that you've got the roof, walls, and windows covered, and I don't want to slow this whole thing down. I thought about it last night, and maybe you should hire some extra hands for some of the other things. You know what needs doing. I trust you."

What the fuck? I thought I would have had an uphill battle, despite her seeing me so unhinged during our argument yesterday. "So that's it?"

"It's best that I'm not around, anyway. I'd just get in the way."

If you did, I wouldn't mind. Whoa! Where'd that thought

come from? As quickly as it had, however, I pushed it out of my head. "Okay." She stopped at her vehicle and stood with the door open, looking as if she had something else to say, but she remained silent. "Have a safe trip." She nodded, leaning into the van to drop her duffle bag on the passenger seat before getting behind the wheel. Next thing I knew, she cranked the old beater and peeled out of the driveway as if the hounds of hell were on her tail.

Well that wasn't awkward.

With a bit of relief, I watched the remnant of crushed rock dust dissipate, rubbing between my pecks at the burning sensation I felt there. She was running. I had used that tactic more than once or twice in my life. It's too bad I hadn't done just that before she did. It might have hurt less.

For that brief moment she'd bumped into me, all I had wanted to do was cradle the back of her head, fuse my lips to hers, and taste her over and over again.

"You're no good for her, dumbass," I mumbled as I slid the key Morgan had left me the other day into the lock and turned to hear the deadbolt's click.

Morgan's scent engulfed me as I let myself inside. Her words from yesterday played as if on a loop in my mind. *I think I can figure out what's good and what's not...I'm a grown-ass woman.*

One thing was certain, when Morgan got back, she and I needed to talk.

CHAPTER 13

By the time I finished with my loose ends in the kitchen, it was time to tackle the rest of the demolition in Morgan's bedroom. Nothing could be done with the kitchen until the inspector showed up anyhow, and the crew I had set up for tomorrow had been called to confirm that they would be on site first thing in the morning.

As I walked through the room's threshold, Morgan's scent, stronger this time, invaded me: the one of woman and a subtlety of honeysuckle.

Moving her furniture to the inside wall of her room, surprised that Morgan had helped out by clearing a lot of her belongings from the room on her own, I set to work for the next hour.

The last remnants of daylight had disappeared by the time I'd tackled her office. She'd cleared out that one for me, too.

I wiped at my forehead using the hem of my shirt and sighed. Had Morgan not started her demolition spree the day before, I would have been working well into the wee hours of the morning just to get things ready for the men tomorrow. Instead, I was able to go home and actually relax before falling into bed.

With one last assessing look, I turned and left. Tomorrow was going to be one hell of a day, and her home would be open to the elements for a certain period of time before the roof could be complete with new shingles, not to mention the new windows.

CHAPTER 14

By the time the weekend arrived, I was exhausted from my days at Morgan's, but also motivated to put in some time and work on my own property.

With my brother on loan from his family for the day, bringing reinforcements in the way of my father, I was going to use all the help they were willing to dish out. If I was lucky, I'd be able to get the floor in the kitchen prepped for tile, and the few full joist replacements throughout the rest of the main floor done. How's that for ambition?

"So how's *TL* doing?" Paxton asked as he sucked back his beer while we sat on the front porch with our lunch.

I shrugged my shoulders. "Good, I guess. It's been constant."

"I guess?" Dad's eyebrow rose. "We haven't seen or heard from you since I broke in and your mother nursed you while you were sick."

"I've been busy," I defended. "My latest client is being a tad difficult." There was no way I was bringing up my attraction toward Morgan or the fucked up way we were linked to one another. That would just invite a slew of disapprovals and snide comments from my father and I really didn't need that today.

After Dad left, Paxton stopped drilling screws into the subflooring board he was securing and turned to me. "So dish. What's been going on with you?"

"What do you mean?"

"Don't play coy," he said. "You look like you haven't slept in days and when Dad asked you questions earlier, it seemed like you were giving him the runaround."

I groaned. "What is this, the Grand Inquisition?"

"I know something's up, T."

I sighed. "It's just the job. I'm working on a large project, a total facelift and then some."

"Yeah, that's not it." Paxton sized me up and continued. "There's more to it than that."

"What's it matter?" I asked. "A woman asked me to do some work on her house after it was flooded."

He chuckles. "A woman! Now we're getting some-where."

Groaning, I flipped him the bird. "Fuck off. Do you want to know the story or not?"

He rolled his eyes. "Go ahead."

I told Paxton about Morgan, her house woes, and the fact that not only had I gotten a large job that would generate funding that would keep me going for the next six months, but that I had also inherited an apprentice of sorts.

The man laughed. "So she wants you to teach her how to fix things?"

Shrugging, I said, "Basically," and found total concentration on the joist I was reinforcing.

"Bro, you can stare at that screw all day, it isn't going to screw itself, you know." His voice held far too much humor. "There's something more with this chick, isn't there?"

"What makes you say that?"

"Well, that hitch in your voice for one proves it, and you haven't been able to look me straight in the eyes since you started talking about the specifics of that job. You're inter-ested in her, aren't you?"

"It doesn't matter. Morgan's untouchable." I wasn't about to let my brother know that despite the fact I labeled her as such, that I had definitely done some touching, and it hadn't been as thorough as I would have liked.

"Morgan…" Paxton rolled her name off his tongue, trying it on for size. "You mean your neighbour, the one Mom bumped into the other day?"

I ran my hand through my hair and huffed. "Christ, I forgot how fast news travels around here."

"When Mom's got something to do with it, yeah, you know it." He laughed, his gaze one of understanding. I could see the wheels turning in that head of his. "So why is she untouchable?"

I knew he wasn't going to leave it alone, but I had to get him to drop it. "P, there're so many reasons I shouldn't go there, so let's just leave it, okay?" I snapped.

"Yeah, yeah." He turned back to his work and said over his shoulder, "You know I'm here to talk to if you need it, right?"

"Yeah, I know."

CHAPTER 15

By late Sunday morning, the joists were stable, the sub-floor was down, my kitchen and entryway tile was on order. While I could have taken some time to relax and enjoy my weekend accomplishments, I found myself in the front yard, tending to some outdoor chores, instead of getting started on installing the main floor carpeting, since the weather was so nice.

I managed to clear the overgrown rose and other assorted bushes and weeds from the gardens, but not without a few battle wounds from the deadwood and sharp thorns. Hell, I'm sure an untamed barn cat would have done far less damage, what with the way my forearms looked.

Backing up a few dozen feet, I took in the look of the front of my house. Despite the serious need for some scraping and paint, the place was now looking more like a neglected home as opposed to a condemned one.

Time for the lawn. I was going to need my brother's riding mower at the length the grass was at.

Paxton and I had just finished loading the mower into the back of his truck when I saw someone making their way up the drivewayon foot.

When the tailgate was put in place, my brother turned around to see where my eyes were aimed, and emitted a low whistle. The sight of a tight white tank top and faded cut-offs that bared legs that seemed a mile long made my heart race, and a knot formed in my throat.

"Wow!" Morgan said, still at a distance.

"Morgan Smyth?" Paxton blurted out.

"You know her?" I turned to my brother, keeping things quiet, since she was still out of earshot.

He nodded. "Yeah, she does some floral work for Allie every now and again, but I've never seen this version of her. What's she doing here?" I ignored his question, my eyes turning back to the woman quickly approaching. Damn, she was hot, but what the hell was she doing back so soon?

"Hey, Pax." She graced him with a grin.

He nodded. "What are you doing here?"

"We're neighbours," Morgan said at the same time I replied with, "She's a client."

"Well, both really." Her gaze trailed me from bottom to top, stopping to meet my eyes and holding them for a moment. My gaze wandered to her lips when her pink tongue jetted out to moisten them.

Some time passed before I heard Paxton clear his throat. "Okay then." I turned to look at him briefly before glancing in Morgan's direction again. "I'll see you in a few hours, right?"

"Yeah," I said, unable to break the connection I had with the woman in front of me. "Need me to bring anything?"

He laughed. "Just your appetite." My head snapped in my brother's direction as he opened the driver's side door. "Behave." I gave him the stink eye when he winked at me, only to turn to face Morgan, witnessing a subtle blush fading. "Good to see you again, Morgan. Stop by some time. You know it doesn't always have to be about business, right?" The woman nodded. "Later, T."

"What are you doing here?" I asked as Paxton's truck turned down the road and kicked up some rocks when he hit the accelerator hard.

"I wanted to apologize for how I was on Thursday. And thank you."

"It's what you hired me to do."

"You were right, though."

"About?"

"The house does look much more authentic with your design." I nodded. "I mean, I knew it would by the drawings, but seeing it in the light of day…"

Seconds trickled by and nothing more was said. Awkwardness rolled around us as we evidently had both chosen to ignore the proverbial elephant in the room.

"Listen," she started. "I–"

"Morgan, I can't talk right now," I snapped. "I need to get myself cleaned up and get to my brother's."

"Right." Was she disappointed? "Well, I'll see you tomorrow then." She turned and started to make her way back down where she'd come from.

"Ah, fuck," I mumbled, and my feet took action. "Morgan, wait." I set my hand on her shoulder.

Bowing her head, she said, "We need to talk," then turned to face me, her eyes never quite meeting mine.

I cleared the lump in my throat as she stepped forward. "I know." I looked down at her.

"We can't ignore what happened, Theo."

"No, we can't." I would have loved to say that we could, just to avoid the damning conversation that would most likely have her hate me, not to mention possibly fire me, but I couldn't.

Morgan's hands landed on my chest as she drew closer and I groaned. This woman was going to kill me long before my time. For a tiny sprite, she sure knew how to turn me inside out by just breathing. My hands moved to her hips and held her in place as we stood there, looking at each other.

"Theo?"

"Hmm?"

In a split second, her hands wrapped themselves around my neck, pulling me in for a kiss I should have put a stop to, but once again, didn't. I chose to ignore all of the red flags inside my head, waving reminders of how I would ruin her, that I wasn't worthy. I was too far gone, too lost in the feel of the tiny woman I held against me—her smell, her taste, the peace being around her brought to my soul.

"Thank you," she whispered against my lips before giving me a quick peck and backing away. I let my arms fall away from her, dumbfounded by what had just transpired, as she walked past me and back to where she'd come from.

I turned to follow her progress, entranced by the sway of her hips, her golden, almost white hair flowing in the breeze.

Letting out a long breath, I willed my heart to slow, my breathing to calm, not to mention my dick to go down. My eyes stayed on Morgan until she'd reached the end of the drivewayand turned to wave. Waving back, I could no longer ignore the truth. This wasn't regular attraction I was feeling. If it was, I would have been able to keep her away. There was more to Morgan and me, and that more was something I apparently couldn't control.

You're royally fucked now, buddy.

CHAPTER 16

I parked the truck in Paxton's driveway and found myself tackled by a rambunctious six-year-old Jasper.

"Hey, buddy." I ruffled my nephew's hair as he clung to my waist.

"Where's Morgan?"

"Your dad's worse than your grandmother," I grumbled.

"Mommy Allie says that you two make a great couple."

My eyes rolled. "And she would know," I said under my breath.

"Huh?"

"Never mind." I gave the kid a light pat on his back.

Jasper led me by the hand up the steps, through the front door, and toward the commotion in the kitchen where I knew everyone was congregated.

As we passed by the den, I spotted Alissa on the phone. She stood sideways to me and startled, her eyes widening when she saw me standing there in the entranceway to the room.

The woman was up to something if that blush of hers was anything to go by. Testing my theory, I crossed my arms and leaned my shoulder onto the wall, my brow arched as I listened in.

"Uh, huh…yeah…It's okay," she said in a hushed tone. "Listen, maybe next time…Yeah. Well, he's here." Her blush deepened. My brother was right. Alissa was cute when she grew shy. "You sure you don't want to pop on by?" She paused to listen to the person on the end of the phone. "Okay…okay, I got it…Like I said, next time."

She turned her back to put the phone back on its cradle and took a deep breath.

"How's Morgan?" I asked.

She spun around, her mouth dropped. "How'd–"

"I had my suspicion, but you just confirmed it." Pushing off the wall, I moved toward her. "Listen, I don't need you playing match-maker, all right?"

"I thought you liked her?"

"I do. I mean, she's a client, she's nice and all…" *make that sexy and frustrating, and I'm all kinds of wrong for her.* If my rambling continued, I would be providing her with enough ammunition to keep doing what I had just advised her not to. So I stopped talking.

"So?"

I ran my hand through my hair and down my face. I had to stop this. "Listen, Allie. I know you think you're doing something good here, but I just can't."

"I'm not doing anything."

"Right." I straightened my stance and my eyes told her to prove my suspicions wrong.

"I just thought…"

"It doesn't matter. Morgan's a client. That's all it can ever be."

"Sure." She walked up to me, her eyes softening. Squeezing my arm with sisterly tenderness, she made to study my face. "Listen, I may not know all that you've been through, but it doesn't take a genius to figure out that it's been a tough go for you, and I'm sure my assessment is grossly understated. But Theo, you shouldn't let what you've been through get in the way of your happiness. Life's too short."

The woman retracted her hand and snuck past me, heading straight for the commotion in the kitchen.

I made to follow, only for the boisterous noise of my family to subside and leave us all surrounded with nothing but silence. I looked at the faces staring back at me. Alissa looked indifferent and avoided my gaze by mooning over her daughter. Paxton looked between his wife and me with confusion, which was quickly replaced by a sly grin. Mom seemed a little overly cheerful, and Dad was just typical Dad with his stoic and unreadable expression.

"Cut the crap guys," I said and pointed at my brother. "I know he told you what he thinks is going on."

"I think it's fantastic!" Mom clapped her hands together as she approached to give me a hug. "I should have known when I saw her bringing you soup the other day."

"You should have seen them this afternoon." Paxton's grin only widened. "She's not just your client, and I think you're underplaying how you feel about her."

"Pax." Allie turned a warning gaze onto her husband.

"Leave the man alone, you two." I couldn't recall the last time my father had taken my side. I guess times have changed. "He's a grown man, he can make his own mind up about women. God only knows he's been around enough of them to know what he wants."

Okay, so maybe they hadn't changed that much, because there it was; the disapproving jab that was covered by sarcasm. He hadn't lost his touch, only finessed it. The man covered it up enough to know that only I would sense the sting, but one look toward Paxton told me that he'd caught on to our father's antics.

"No different than how I was back then, Dad," he said.

"Yeah, but–"

"Dad," he warned.

"Let's just drop it, all right?" I approached my sister-in-law. "Now, how's my beautiful princess?" I took the baby from her arms and cradled her in mine. "You're just as beautiful as your mama, you know that?" I nuzzled the fine hair that met her hairline and inhaled the baby powder scent. She was so tiny, so innocent.

The minuscule body I held in my arms made it hard to believe that those I had fought against had once been as innocent as she was. My mood darkened with the sheer memory of what I'd witnessed in my time away. Kids being used as weapons. Tiny soldiers that ended lives, including their own, for a cause they were told to believe in, but didn't truly understand.

I hadn't noticed Abigail's squirming or the plaintive sounds she emitted until Paxton's hand squeezed my arm. "You okay, bro?"

Feeling the shakes coming on, my vision fading in its periphery, I nodded. "Here, take her." I handed him his daughter. "I need some air."

Looking over at my mother whose gaze was filled with concern, then my father who was studying me, I avoided Alissa's gaze and rushed out the back door, ignoring my family's pleas that I stay and talk.

CHAPTER 17

My appetite had left, the urge to run had hit, and loneliness had set in. I wondered how long it would be before someone came out to find me by the man-made pond. The view of the setting sun fading behind the treeline of the woods that backed my brother's property helped me center myself and regain some semblance of control over my thoughts.

Leaning forward with my elbows on my knees, I sensed Paxton's presence. Without turning, a humorless laugh escaped me. "Seems like yesterday you and me were fighting over Suzie Quincy."

"You should see her now." Paxton dropped to the bench beside me, leaning back.

I peered at him from the corner of my eye. "Still hot?"

"Not." I chuckled at the face he made. Silence stemmed between us, only interrupted by the sounds of nature. "What happened back there?"

I let out a loud breath and felt myself deflate. Bowing my head, I shook it from side to side. "Old memories."

"You know you can tell me anything, right?"

"It's not that easy, P."

He pointed out the obvious. "You kind of freaked everyone out back there. I think we…No, *I* deserve to know what's going on with you, T. One minute you're holding Abbie like she's precious cargo, and the next, the look on your face–"

My temper flared. "What?"

"If looks couldn't kill, your grip on her surely would have done it eventually."

"What are you saying? You don't want me around your kids? I can't say that I blame you."

Paxton cut me off. "That's not what I'm saying at all and you know it! Stop jumping down my throat. I'm not Dad. In case you haven't noticed, Jasper worships the ground you walk on and Abigail…" He groaned his frustration. "You've been out of our lives long enough. It's time for you to get out of that rut of yours."

"And how do you suppose I do that, huh?" Rage overwhelmed me and I shot to my feet, keeping my back to him. "You have no fucking idea what you're talking about."

"You're right, I don't. So why don't you explain it to me?"

I turned sharply to face him and my rage dissipated to a manageable level. *Maybe I should.*

Something told me that if anyone would understand where I was coming from, outside of the military, it would be my brother. Paxton wouldn't judge me; if anything, he'd defend me like he always has.

My voice came out sounding hoarse. "The things I saw, the things I did over there, P…" I swallowed the ever-growing lump in my throat. "No one should go through that."

"I think we can both agree that everyone here at home knows that you've seen and done things that are far from honorable to make ends meet, things that chip away at the humanity inside of you."

I nodded and met his gaze, mine hardening. "You're right." Gritting the next words through my teeth, I asked, "Tell me, little brother, have you ever taught Jasper how to use a gun?"

"What's this got to–" He clued in almost immediately as to what caused my earlier behavior and his mouth snapped shut.

"What would you do, how would you deal, if your son

turned around on you with an automatic rifle and shot your family to death in front of your eyes, all because it was a rite of passage, a proof of his loyalty?

"How would you feel if you had to turn the gun on some kid no bigger than Jasper in self-defence, to protect your men? What about if your brother, your father, your mother even, approached you as if welcoming you home only to blow you and everyone within a hundred meters to smithereens?"

The more I went on, the easier it got to purge the atrocities I had come to witness. "How about watching your friends, your brothers and sisters-in-arms die in front of your very eyes? Or not knowing if you're going to make it to the next day, and breathing each breath as if it might be your last? We're all trained and we know the risks we're taking, but it doesn't really sink in until you're over there, bro.

"You know what's worse? It's knowing that you've failed those that you've sworn to protect and bring back to their families safely. *Sorry* doesn't cut it when you fuck up over there, Paxton." I swallowed hard, trying to keep my emotions from taking over. "Failing means casualties. It messes with your head. My superiors only care about one thing, and it sure isn't those that serve beneath them. We're all dispensable to them, unless we have something they want. I found out a little too late, though, that the final outcome of the mission was the only thing they were after. It's all about them winning their latest pissing match.

"I lived all of that, little brother." I took a deep breath. "I lost too many friends, friends I swore to protect. They had my six and they thought I had theirs. Only, I failed them. I'm no good. I'm not the man that you, Mom, Dad, or anyone else thinks I am. I'm not deserving to stand here. I should have died over there along with the parts of me that did dozens of times–"

"You're right where you need to be, Theodore Lowell."

I spun around. "Dad?"

"Get that shit out of your head, son. You did what you were supposed to do over there. What you were trained to do. What you were ordered. You keep ignoring the fact that you weren't the one to get them in that explosion. You didn't set those charges. Sure, they died, and you lived. It's a tough pill to swallow, and I imagine even tougher because you were their leader at the time, and their friend."

"Dad…" Paxton shook his head.

Our father held his hand up. "No, Paxton, let me finish. Theodore, I never got to tell you this ten years ago, and because of our issues, we never spoke until you came back to us. I might have disagreed with a lot of things you've done over the years, but I've never been prouder of you or the man you've become since you enlisted."

"What…a killer?" I noted the obvious. "I'm sure as fuck not a hero like all you folks here paint me to be."

"I never said you were," he said. "But whether you see yourself as one or not, others do. You've done more than most of us can ever do. You say you've failed, but all I see is a man who's been broken by the unfortunate events that war brings. You're no more half of a man than I am. If anything, you're more deserving of a happy life than most of us because you know the value of it. You know freedom, and the fight it takes to keep it.

"Your grandfather went to war and he never came back. It hurt like hell to lose him when I was a teenager, but it hurt worse to lose you, son. The worst part about all of this is that you're here, but you're not. You may be here physically, but you're still lost."

The man had a point.

"Dad's right, T," Paxton said. "They died, but you didn't. You owe them your life, but think on it. If you had died, do you think they would have stopped living? Do you think Rick wouldn't have gone back to his life and lived it, that the others would have turned their backs on their families?"

I had heard those words from the shrinks I had met with over the years, my superiors, the team members in my ops. None of it registered until now. None of it meant anything because those who'd uttered the words before hadn't meant a thing to me.

"You need to get back in there, son, your mother's worried about you," Dad said.

"I'll be there in a few." The man nodded and turned to leave. As he walked away from Paxton and me, my mouth opened and without thinking, I blurted out, "Dad?" He paused mid-step and turned to face me. "Thanks." All he did was nod, his lips in a flat line, grief present in his eyes, before he continued his trek for the house.

I sighed, my shoulders slumping as I looked at my feet.

Paxton broke the lingering silence. "You know…I don't think I've ever heard him go on like that before."

I snorted. "No shit. And when he ever had anything to say, he was usually giving us shit for something we did or didn't do."

"Right." For a long moment, neither of us said anything. "For what it's worth, I'm sorry, T."

My head snapped up and looked at my brother. "For what?"

"For the shit that you were put through while we grew up. It's what made you leave in the first place. And I'm sorry for what happened to your team…and to you."

I nodded. "What I said," we began to walk back, "it wasn't the half of it."

"You'll tell me when you're ready." He slapped me on the back. "Right now, we have some food to eat, kids to entertain, and your mood to brighten up."

I was all for it, but I wondered how the hell we'd manage that last item. "It's all so easy for you, isn't it?"

"It's never been easy." He gave me a pointed look. "And I know it'll be even harder to get you living again like you once did."

"I've changed, P. After what I've been through, there's no way I could go back to the way I was."

"And maybe Morgan can help you with that."

"About Morgan." My feet stopped moving.

My brother followed suit and halted in front of me.

"What's that guilty look about? Something happened, didn't it?"

"Uh, yeah, about that…Nothing can happen between us."

"Why not? By the way she blushed earlier, and the way you looked as if you were starved, I'd say that plenty of good could happen there."

"But it can't," I stated.

"Again, I'm asking you *why*."

I was going to have to come out and say it and that admission sent anger flaring through me. If it weren't for that one horrible fact, I might have entertained exploring my attraction toward her, employee-employer status be damned. "Because I let her brother get killed over there, all right!" I shouted.

The look on my brother's face could have told a story in itself. It certainly hadn't been a piece of information that he expected. "You knew Steve?"

I nodded. "Except he went by Damon."

"Wow, now that's all kinds of fucked up."

"You're telling me."

"How'd you find out?"

"The day Morgan called about her leak. We were in her room and I saw a picture…" As we started for the house again, I explained all about Damon, aka, Steve. Paxton took in every parcel of information I dished out, lapping it up like a starved kitten.

"I can't be with her when I know I've just as well killed her brother." Paxton tried to cut me off. "Don't tell me it's not my fault. I'm not stupid, Pax. It doesn't change the fact that I led that convoy that day. It was me who analyzed the intel, me who had the lead, who made the decision that sent us all to our deaths. Hell, Morgan doesn't even know the whole story, she only knows that her brother and I served together and that I was there the day she lost him. But when I do tell her the details, because I owe her that much, I'll be lucky to still be alive when I get done."

"You don't honestly think she'd blame you for

that, do you?" he asked as we climbed the stairs to the patio.

I shrugged. "I don't know what to think anymore. But there's one thing I do know, and that's the last thing she needs is for me to hurt her more when she discovers I played a part in changing her life for the worse three years ago."

"I don't think she'll see it that way," he said. "But all I can say is, do what you think is right."

The problem was that doing what was right and what felt right were two entirely different things.

As we walked through the French doors, Allie handed Abigail to me despite my protest. "Take her or I'll drop her." That was threat enough for me.

"I'm sorry, princess," I whispered, kissing the little hand that reached out for me. I let her curl her digits around my large finger and she graced me with a toothless grin. "Your uncle's got some things he needs to figure out."

Well, that was the understatement of the decade.

CHAPTER 18

Nerves got the better of me this morning as I paused at the top of Morgan's front steps.

If I were to say that all of what my father and brother had voiced to me yesterday hadn't struck a chord, I'd be lying. Now, more than ever, I was confused about what I should do.

True, I owed Morgan an explanation as to what had happened to her brother, mostly in the effort to make her understand why things couldn't go any further between us. But then there was the selfish part of me that wanted to seize what I wanted for the first time since that horrible day, to see where things went between us. Hell, with two simple kisses I knew all too well how hot things could be between Morgan and I. But heat and passion were only a blip on the radar for what I wanted out of life…out of *her*. And wasn't that the kicker! The one girl to catch my eye, to tug at my heartstrings, was the one I shouldn't have anything to do with. But then again, going with my mother's words from years ago, *the heart wants what it wants.*

Watching families torn apart by the loss of their loved ones had me wanting a life I never thought I'd want. Until *that* day, I had been happy to hang with the boys and take solace in the form of a willing woman who could make me forget the horrors I had seen for a few short hours. Truth was that those horrors never compared to those that chased me in my everyday life afterward. Morgan seemed to make all of that better somehow.

The front door creaked open. "Theo?" Turning, Morgan

stared at me with question in her eyes. "Is everything all right?"

"Yeah." I forced a smile. "Just a lot on my mind, it's all."

She nodded and moved back to allow me entrance. "You want to talk about it?"

"I don't think we have a choice." I stopped at two arm-chairs that hadn't been taken over by the mess of boxes from her kitchen and dining room and motioned for her to sit.

Letting herself drop in to one of the chairs, she sighed. "Look, what happened the other day–"

"And yesterday," I added, staying on my feet.

Her eyes narrowed, but she nodded. "And yesterday." Her tone was sharp. "I'm sorry."

She was sorry?

"Don't be," I found myself saying. "I started it, and I shouldn't have. I work for you. Hell, I don't know what you do, but you work with my sister-in-law in whatever capacity that you do. I'm your neighbour." I sighed. All those reasons sounded like complete bullshit to my own ears, so I gave her the truth. "Hell, I got your brother killed, Morgan." *Nice way of easing into things, dumbass!*

"What!"

"You heard me." I kept my eyes to the floor like a shamed child. "Your brother was driving that night, Morgan. I was his leader. I should have known. I was supposed to have their sixes. All of them."

"Oh my God." She held her hand to her mouth, her eyes filling with tears. I couldn't take my gaze off of her, feeling the need to watch what the truth did to her, to wear my shame as properly as I should have, and the only way I could do that was to take in every nuance of hurt I bestowed upon her.

So I'm a masochist, sue me.

And in true masochistic fashion, I did the asshole thing. I told Morgan the entire story.

"Damon and Tiny were in the front. Rick and I were in the back. We survived the blast but then he and–"

"You..." her voice was riddled with unshed emotion.

"You said you were there, but…"

I nodded. "It's my fault. It was a roadside bomb. Damon and Tiny died instantly, I'm sure of it. My leg was broken in the chaos before Donnelly and I were captured," I explained as I paced the floor in front of her. "After they took me, I was beaten and tortured for information. I could hear Rick's screams from a room down the hall from me. There was nothing I could do. When they came and rescued me, I'd been praying for death, but what kept me alive was knowing that Rick was alive too. I only found out afterward that he hadn't made it. That the screams I'd heard…They weren't his. Fuck, Morgan, they weren't *his*!"

I crouched down so I could look her in the eyes, the look of terror there was my doing. There was no way I could be around her without seeing that look at every turn. It would only prove what I'd known all this time: I was a failure, a murderer…and no good for anyone. "Now you know why nothing can happen between us." I got up to leave. "I also don't think it would be wise to keep working for you. I have guys that can do the job just as well as I can. I'm sure they wouldn't mind teaching you about the trade, either. I just…can't."

"So you keep saying." She got up to approach me. I backed up. Suddenly, the little sprite didn't look so little anymore. I sort of understood how that hulk of an insurance contractor might have felt a few weeks back. She dominated the space surrounding us. "So was agreeing to work for me, to teach me, some kind of a pity deal?"

I groaned, but not at her line of question, more because of her proximity. The woman had my back against the wall, literally.

"In case you've forgotten, you're paying me."

"Still! No contractor would have agreed to teach a little lady a thing or two about construction."

"I'm not just any contractor."

Her hand came up a fraction too quick and my reflexes kicked in, programmed to avoid any kind of striking. I grabbed her wrist and held it, my thumb finding the soft pad of skin over her pulse point. Her other hand came up slower and her fingers played over the stubble on my jaw. "No, you're not." Her front pressed to mine.

I swallowed hard. "Morgan."

"We have a contract." She backed away, her demeanour changing from seductress to cool and business-like. "You will honor that contract."

"Fine," I spat, not sure if what I felt was relief that she wanted me to stay or not. "If that's all, I'd like to get my day started."

"Fine by me." Her hands clenched and released repeatedly at her sides. Before anything else could be said on either part, I moved away from her, grabbed my tool belt, which I'd left by the front entrance, and went to work.

CHAPTER 19

A week went by, an excruciating one at that, where instructions were given and followed methodically. Morgan followed my lead, but pretty much kept her distance. We rarely spoke when we were in the same room together unless it was about the work being done on her house. At first, I thought it was a good thing. But as the days flew by, I missed the times where one of us would make a crack about something which would make the other laugh. I missed her easygoing nature.

To be honest, if Morgan wasn't working on the house, she was always outside in her gardens, tending to her flowers. Today was one of those days. I sat on the back patio eating my lunch while watching her go back and forth between her gardens, to her greenhouses, then her barn with freshly cut blooms. It was no wonder she always smelled of flowers.

As if she sensed my watching her, she turned and her gaze met mine.

"You need something?" The peacefulness of the countryside was interrupted by swinging hammers, drills, and compressors as the crew still worked on the outside components of Morgan's house. I also had a few men working in her kitchen. They were working on the drywall today.

"The guys will be done with the drywall in the kitchen today. I wanted to show you what I've done with your cabinets, if you're not too busy." I shoved the last bite of my sandwich into my mouth.

She tried to keep the look of excitement off of her features, but I caught it. "When?"

"Well, I'm done my lunch, so any time. You should probably eat something first, though."

"Fine." The woman sauntered past me, heading for the house, a bit more of a bounce to her step, which had me smiling. It was the first time I'd gotten a glimpse of happiness of some sort from her since our talk on Monday.

I was busy thoroughly inspecting the finish on the final cabinet when I heard Morgan's gasp.

"Those are my cabinets?" She stopped to stand beside me, laying a hand on the freshly stained and lacquered wooden box.

"M-hmm." I was rather pleased at how they'd turned out. Even the one cabinet whose doors had been ripped off looked as good as new.

"Theo, they're beautiful." Morgan's hand touched my arm and it all came back to me. The heat. The want. The unseen force that kept pulling me toward her. The one I hadn't felt this week, maybe because, until then, I hadn't realized that we hadn't touched each other all week.

Stumbling over my words, I rambled. "I think they turned out all right. Are you sure you like them this color? I can always–"

"Theo, stop!" My gaze finally met hers. "They're exactly what I wanted. Thank you for doing this."

Seeing the brightness of her smile had my mouth going dry, so I just nodded.

"Are the doors done?"

"Yeah, they're over here." In order to show her, I had to move away from her, which meant her hand no longer touched me. The instant I did so, I felt the loss of warmth. But it would be worth it when she saw what came next.

"Oh my God! What did you do?" Morgan exclaimed.

I stood back as she inspected the doors. They'd been simple cabinet doors once. Yesterday, after hearing her talk with Alissa about their current project, seeing the love she had for her business, the love that had been passed down from her grandmother, I had made a slight change to her original plans.

Each door was plain with their mitered edges, but now, in the center of each, I'd taken a stencil I'd drawn up with a fancy filigree vine, and with the help of a handheld router and chisel as well as a wood burning tool, I'd added the template to each surface. It was delicate, but also made the cabinets one of a kind. I'd only done it for the uppers.

"You did this?" Morgan turned to me, her eyes filled with unshed tears.

I moved to stand beside her, brushing my hand over part of the detailing. To be honest, they'd turned out a hell of a lot better than I expected. "Yeah."

"When did you have time?"

I didn't want to tell her that since we'd agreed on our new working arrangement, I hadn't had much luck with sleeping, so I'd taken up the habit of coming back to her place and working until the early hours of the morning, only going home to clean up, take a quick nap and head back to work. I shrugged. "I guess with the extra help around here…"

Morgan's hand covered mine, and she moved closer. I avoided her gaze, keeping mine set on the dainty pattern my hand was still covering.

"Theo?" Her voice shook.

"Hmm?"

"Theo…look at me." I shook my head in response. "Why won't you look at me?" I bit my lip. There were too many reasons why. "Then tell me, why would you do this?"

"Because I knew you'd love it." I shrugged, whispering the next. "I wanted to give you something beautiful for all the ugliness I've caused." I finally met her gaze, head-on.

And then it happened again.

Leaning onto her toes, Morgan moved her hands so they ran up to stop over my chest. The magnetic pull between us was stronger than ever, but I forced my arms to stay at my sides. I didn't know what would happen if I touched her.

One of her hands reached behind my neck and pulled me down. I told myself I wouldn't let things get this far again. But would another taste be so wrong? By the time that thought occurred, however, Morgan's lips were pressed softly against mine in a series of sweet kisses. And when her tongue traced the seam of my lips, I was so lost in savoring our connection that I opened for her for a more thorough taste.

All too soon, Morgan pulled away, leaving my brain a jumbled mess. My hand cupped her cheek, fingers feeling the soft edges of her features before I finally stepped back. "You're welcome, Morg." With that, I walked out of the garage, leaving her to her thoughts and emotions.

CHAPTER 20

This weekend, Ben rallied us all together to help him out with a fencing project. It was clear as day that he was lost when it came to Hannah. You know that dream most women will have of the white picket fence? Well, we were building it. I just didn't expect an entire flock of women to show up, but then again, why wouldn't they when their men were hard at work.

What shocked me most was that Morgan showed up with Alissa.

After yesterday's cabinet revelation and the ensuing kiss, Morgan and I hadn't said anymore to one another. I'd caught her eyeing me from time to time, but if I'm being honest, I was just as guilty of doing the same thing. The woman I should avoid at all cost, but couldn't, took hold of my every waking thought. She also haunted my dreams in the most delicious, yet tortuous of sensual ways too.

I had gone to the backyard to rinse myself off with the hose when I felt her presence. Then the gentle pressure of her hands on my bare back had me freezing. "You shouldn't." I was losing ground here, and fast, as Morgan's lips met the skin between my shoulder blades.

"Theo–"

I stepped away, turning to face her. Her hair was up high in a messy pony tail, but instead of her shorts and tank top, today she wore a simple yellow sundress. She looked innocent, and in that moment, I wanted to be the one to sully that angel-like image of hers.

"I should get back," I said after a lengthy moment of staring at one another. "The guys are bound to start asking questions."

"Yeah." Morgan's smile was forced.

"See you on Monday?"

"Yeah…Monday" is what I heard as I rushed for the front yard.

Well, Monday arrived, and with some help, I got Morgan's kitchen cabinets installed. But then the day went to shit and nothing worked according to plan.

Working in close proximity with Morgan all day was wearing thin on me after our brief interactions of last Friday and Saturday. Combine my sexual and emotional frustration with my lack of sleep, and there's a recipe for disaster.

Sure, Morgan was learning how to do the basics of renovations like drywall, plastering, and then some, but every little instruction on my part had been short and sweet in an effort to get her further away from me before I did something epically stupid. Like pinning-her-to-the-wall-and-having-my-way-with-her stupid. Suffice to say, the air grew thick with sexual tension, bordering on hostile, and things finally came to blows between us for the second time in under a week.

"Get out of here and let me do my work, will you! I know you have other things to do," I snapped. "Go pick the damn paint colors and your kitchen backsplash or something…just get out."

Despite my snippy comments throughout the day, Morgan didn't balk at my attitude. Until now. "Why? You're the one who asked me if I wanted to know how to do framing and install drywall," she spat as she turned toward me with a two-by-four. "Can't stand the sight of the poor little bereaved sister whose brother you killed?"

My jaw dropped. I wanted to shout that I hadn't killed him, but I didn't. The fact of the matter was that she was right. She had a right to be mad, to say those things. I deserved it, especially with the way I was behaving. But it didn't mean I had to take it.

"Get the fuck out of here, Morgan!" I growled and took the wood from her as she turned and bent over to grab another piece.

"No!" she yelled back as she twirled, but I missed the fact that she was ahead of me with another two-by-four. As she swung, time slowed and I saw the wood flying toward me with no time to react. By the time I tried to dodge, it was making hard contact with the back of my head.

Next thing I knew I was on the floor. "Fuck!" I tried to focus my vision through the dark spots that clouded it.

The board clattered to the floor right before Morgan came to kneel down beside me. "Shit, Theo! Are you okay?"

"What do you think?" I tried to sit up.

"Stay still."

I waved my hand in dismissal to keep her away from me. "I'll be fine."

"No." She flattened her palm on my chest, forcing me to stay where I was. "You might be concussed."

"Takes a harder hit than that to keep me down." I lifted my hand to rub the back of it. *Son of a bitch that hurt!* It came away with a bit of blood on my fingertips.

"Shit!" Morgan got up and ran to the bathroom. By the time she made her way back to me, I had gotten up to my feet only for the room to start spinning. "I told you to stay still, damn it!"

I grabbed onto her forearm to steady myself and walked slowly toward the bed. "I'll be fine, really." I sat down.

I heard her almost imperceptible mumbling of "Men!" to the ceiling before she sighed, looked down and said, "Just let me clean you up."

Standing between my legs, she cupped the back of my head with the wet cloth. The cool sensation eased some of the pain away, and my eyes fluttered closed with the relief.

When I opened them again, Morgan had tears in her eyes, and I could tell that by the way she bit her bottom lip she was trying damn hard not to break down by focusing her attention on taking care of me.

"Morg?"

"I didn't mean any of what I said," she whispered as the first of her tears spilled. "I just…I don't know." She let out a loud breath.

"It's true," I said dryly. "That's why you said it. I don't blame you for saying it, either."

"It's not and you know it. I was mad. I had no right to say those things."

"You had *every* right," I corrected her. "You more than anyone else." I grabbed her outstretched arm and pulled it and the cloth it held away from my head, but I didn't release her. Instead, I pulled her so she sat down beside me. "You want the truth?"

She snorted. "I wouldn't expect you to start sugar-coating things now."

"Cut the sarcasm for now, would you?"

"Theo." My eyes narrowed. "Okay, I'm sorry."

"The truth…" I began and she nodded to urge me on, "is that even though you're the sister of a man I swore to protect and failed," I grumbled with the next, "you soothe me." Her eyes widened. "I'm only a shell of a man. I have nothing to give. I have hope of having what my brother and parents have some day, but I don't think I'm destined for it, at least not yet. There's something about you, though. At first, I accepted the job because of a sense of guilt and loyalty toward your brother. You both had all of these plans for this place and my actions took that away. It was a way to give back, to give to you what your brother no longer could. But now…"

"Now *what*?"

"It hasn't been that long, but other than soothing me, Morgan, you make me want to be a better man so I can have those things my family and friends have. I don't feel as empty when I'm around you, which is why I'm having a hell of a time keeping things platonic." I shook my head. "I still don't think we should take things further, though." She groaned her annoyance. I huffed and ran my hand through my hair, wincing when my fingers skimmed the goose egg lump that was forming at the back of my skull. "I'm really screwing this up here, aren't I?"

"You're doing fine. Go on."

"You deserve so much better than what I can offer. Your brother's been taken from you. And now you're faced with me, a man who doesn't even know how to live life the way it should be lived." I ran a finger over her cheek, the tip skimming down her cheekbone before cupping the side of her face. "You're young, vibrant, successful, and beautiful. You can do better than me. There's nothing for me to give aside from anything physical, and you shouldn't have to settle for that, and it's not what I want for myself either. I'd be cheating both of us out of something great."

Her expression was unreadable. "I see."

I wiped at her tears with the pad of my thumb. "I've hurt you enough for this lifetime, Morgan. I can't bear to think I could do it again if I can't get over my hang-ups."

"But you are hurting me, Theo. With everything that you've said just now…" I pulled my hand back from her, but she took that opportunity to move closer. Shifting, she knelt in front of me and reached up to cup my face with her hands. "I've listened to you, now you'll give me the same courtesy and listen to me."

"Morgan," I groaned. The visual of her on her knees, between my legs no less, wasn't what I needed right now. "I don't know how much more I can take."

"Then give up, Theo," she said with unmistakable stubbornness. "Because like I've said before, I'm a grown-ass woman and I'm capable of making my own decisions. I'm not asking for forever. I'm asking for you to take a leap of faith and let me show you what kind of man you are. Theo, see yourself through my eyes just for a little while.

"You think that you're only a shell of a man, but what I see is someone who cares, who's been through so much that he's bottled the guilt, the misery and suffering, and being the only survivor, he thinks that he's less than deserving to live. You led a team that day and three out of four of you died. It's sad. It's horrible. My brother was one of them, so I know what that loss feels like, Theo. But you have a family who loves you, one who didn't know you were alive until recently. And you have friends. People care about you, whether you think you deserve it or not. It's not something you get to control. It's something you should cherish.

"You didn't die that day because somehow—someone—something out there had another plan for you. Theo, you came back! Sure, a little banged up, scarred severely inside more than out, but you have a second chance at life and you should take it. You say you failed, and I know you believe it, or else you wouldn't be beating yourself up this much, but I have something to say about that too.

"You never failed your parents. You never failed your brother, your sister-in-law, or niece and nephew. You never failed your friends, and anyone else who supported you from afar. Theo, you didn't fail my brother, nor did you fail your team." Her face drew nearer, but her eyes, determined and filled with conviction, refused to let my gaze wander from hers. She was a fierce one. "And you most certainly never failed me. My brother did come home, Theo, just not the way we all envisioned. I said goodbye, I've been working on my demons, but you have yet to start working on yours. I don't blame you for any of it," she said, and kissed my cheek softly. "I'll never blame you." She kissed my other cheek. "None of it is your fault, Theo." She kissed the side of my mouth before pulling away far enough to make sure our eyes made contact. "Not your–"

I grabbed the back of her head and smashed my lips to hers.

Like a cat, she crawled up and over to settle on my lap, her arms grasping my shoulders. When our tongues met, the taste of her exploded in my mouth and I groaned. The woman was amazing!

Her chest pressed to mine, yet it still wasn't close enough. My arms surrounded her like vices and she took her cue from me as we both sought the closeness only we could provide each other.

By the time we pulled apart, our breathing was laboured and heat radiated off our bodies. I leaned my forehead to hers and closed my eyes, trying to calm my erratic heartbeat.

Something in me opened up. A wall began to crack, letting warmth in as the bricks tumbled away. With three words, tension was further released. Thinking about Paxton's words from over a week ago, I knew what was right. Finally.

"I give up."

CHAPTER 21

The moment I said those three words, the chocolate pools that stared back at me glimmered with tenderness.

"Are you sure?" she asked.

My arms loosened their hold on her and rubbed up and down her upper arms as I studied her face. Pupils dilated, lips swollen from my kisses, a rosy flush to her cheeks—the woman was beautiful. And for some fucked up reason she wanted me. I'd be a fool not to try and find my place in the world, and to chase a possibility at happiness with her.

"I'm not sure I can do this right, or do it at all." I swallowed hard. "But I don't think I can fight what's going on here. Even if I could, somehow, it feels as though it would be a losing battle."

She pecked my lips. "We'll take it slow."

I pushed her hair behind her ears, studying her further, and cupped her face between my palms. "I can't do slow right now, sweetheart."

Morgan's eyes widened as the realization hit that she was sitting over what I would have to dignify as a world-class erection. I laughed at her deer-in-the-headlights expression and pulled her in for another kiss.

Slow and sweet turned into pure unadulterated heat the moment my tongue traced the seam of her lips, and she opened for me on a moan. Her hands rubbed up my chest and over my shoulders as she pulled me tight against her body.

My hand fisted her golden locks and tilted her head back

as I rained kisses down her chin, along her jaw and her throat.

"You smell amazing. Taste so good," I mumbled against the exposed skin above her tank top. She shivered before pulling away, her gaze filled with fire. "I want more." The woman nodded her consent with vehemence.

She leaned in and smashed her lips against mine. "Shirt," she said and bit my lower lip, soothing the sting with her tongue. "Take it off."

Her hands reached for the hem and I helped her pull my t-shirt up and over my head, then Morgan let it drop onto the floor behind her. Cool fingers traced the scars that marred my chest—the ones inflicted by my captors. I reached to pull her hand away, but her lips replaced her digits and I was ensnared by the sweetness that was Morgan.

Her lips left a blazing trail from my markings up to my neck and jaw. She paused to nip and suck on my earlobe, which had me near my breaking point where self-control was concerned.

"You're killing me here, Morg."

She'd giggled before, but never had I heard her sounding so carefree and sexy until now.

Pulling away with a Cheshire cat grin, she grabbed for the hem of her top and pulled it up, revealing the black lace that hid underneath.

"I want your hands, your lips, on me, Theo." She leaned down as if she couldn't get enough of my kisses.

My hands ran up her sides, feeling the heated silken flesh before tracing my thumbs beneath the underwire to her bra. My fingers worked their way toward those two luscious mounds that I ached to touch.

I pulled the lace down, exposing her breasts, her nipples starting to peak. "Beautiful." I squeezed one and took the other in my mouth, flicking my tongue over its tip.

Morgan hissed, her head falling back onto her shoulders, her body arching toward me. "Oh, yes!" Her fingers grabbed my nape and held my head to her breast in a begging act to continue.

I switched to the other, wanting to devote as much attention to it as I had to the first.

Her hips ground hard onto my stiff cock, my jeans feeling unbearable.

"Theo, please." Her voice was hoarse with desire. "I need...*please.*"

I pulled back, blowing on the damp and erect tip. "What do you want, baby?"

"More! I need to feel you," she said, her breathing having gone ragged. Her hand skimmed down my chest. "I need all of it." She cupped me over my jeans and squeezed.

I growled. "In time, sweetheart. I'm far from done with you, yet."

She whimpered.

I picked Morgan up by her ass and twisted around to lay her down in the middle of the mattress, the plastic covering to shield her linens from dust crinkling beneath us. Straddling her thighs, I reached for the button on her shorts at the same time her hands grabbed onto my belt buckle.

I laughed at the determined yet rushed look on her face.

"What?"

I stilled her hands. "Patience."

"But..."

I leaned forward and hovered above her face. "Baby, I'd love nothing more than to whip my dick out and fuck you senseless, right now, but I need to taste you first." I proceeded to kiss her swollen lips as my hand trailed down to cup her heat. "Right here. See if you're just as sinful as that mouth of yours."

The woman's chocolate eyes darkened. "Theo," she said breathless and squeaked when my thumb added pressure to the junction between her thighs, making her squirm.

I smirked. "You're a wildcat in bed, aren't you?" My lips trailed down her body, not caring what her answer was. When I reached her waist, I paused to look up at her. "Take off your bra, Morgan," I ordered as I began to shimmy her shorts down from her hips. She released the front catch to it as she lifted her hips to aid me with stripping her lower half.

"Theo?" Morgan lay bared to me, and I had yet to move from between her legs, transfixed by her sex. When I didn't say anything, I felt her emotionally pull away, soon followed with her attempt at a physical withdrawal.

"Don't move," I growled and reached out to run the back of my fingers over her moist lips, mostly bared, except for a small patch of trimmed hair above her pubic bone. "You're beautiful," I said with reverence. My eyes moved up to meet hers. "All of you, Morgan. Absolutely gorgeous."

"Theo," she whispered and reached for me.

I shook my head and quickly shifted so my face hovered above her pelvis. "Patience," I repeated, trailing a finger through her slit, delighting in the scent of her body wash mixed with the one of unmistakable desire.

I lowered my face, keeping my eyes fused to her bewildered ones.

"Theo!" She cried as my thumbs opened her up and my tongue flicked her clit. "I don't think…"

"Don't think, baby. Just enjoy."

"But–"

"Hasn't anyone…" I let my words trail. She blushed. "Seriously?" She shook her head indicating the negative. "You mean to say–"

"No!" Morgan said exasperated. "No one's eaten me out since *him*, all right? I-I don't taste good, okay? Is that what you want to hear?" I could tell she was embarrassed. Hell, the tension in her body had her strung tight like a bow that was about to snap.

"Baby–"

She shook her head. "Just don't, okay? Let's drop it. I don't need your pity."

"Is that what you think?"

"Well…"

"What I pity are the idiots that never took the time to taste you."

"What?"

I ignored her reply, giving her a lick from bottom to top, twirling my tongue around her nub, and finished off with a quick flick that had her thighs quivering. "Yep, I was right the first time. You're delicious, baby."

It didn't take much to halt her protesting as her hips came up off the mattress, aimed straight for my mouth on my next assault. I took her action as agreement and wrapped my lips around her pearl, sucking her, and pushed a finger into her core.

"Oh!"

Her hips began to ride the combination of my mouth and hand. I pulled away, engrossed in her many faces of bliss and added a second finger.

"Damn, baby." I kissed the inside of her quivering thigh. "You're so close."

"I need you now, Theo," she said between pants.

"Not yet, baby. I want to feel you explode on my tongue."

"No!"

"Yes." I growled, and then latched onto her clit and she collapsed onto her back, fisting her hands in the plastic sheeting as she succumbed to my ministrations. I reached for her sweet spot. "Give in, baby. Give it all to me. I promise I'll take care of you." It's all it took as her body bucked and her flavour coated my tongue on a cry that resonated off the walls.

My cock ached against the zip to my jeans, and I was quick to undo my belt and the like, shoving my pants and underwear down my hips before settling over her body.

By the time I'd reached her face, she pulled my head down to capture my lips with hers.

My length was pushed into the cradle of her thighs and I ground myself against her slickness. It would be so easy to just sink myself inside her.

The thought had my body stiffening. "Fuck," I mumbled against her lips and buried my head in the crook of her neck.

"What is it?" Morgan asked, her fingertips trailing over

my spine.

"Please tell me you have condoms."

She shook her head. "I threw them out after…"

I lifted my head to look at her, brow arched. "Are you saying that you–"

She shook her head. "Not since Richard."

"You can't be serious?"

"Well, yeah. Things weren't…After he…I've been on the pill for years, but I just never trusted him to–"

I fused my lips to hers and pulled away to look her in the eyes. "I don't want to hear about *him*." I kissed her hard again. "We can wait, do other things, until we have condoms. I wouldn't mind another taste of–"

She shook her head. "You're clean?"

I was taken back by her question. I'd never gone without a rubber before, and what was strange was that the thought of doing so didn't bother me in the slightest when it came down to Morgan. "I was given a complete workup before my discharge. I'm clean and I haven't been with anyone since…well, in over three years."

At that moment, her legs lifted and wrapped themselves around my ass where she squeezed me closer to her core. My eyes widened. "Please," she said.

I reached down between us and grabbed my shaft. The hold of her legs slackened a bit and I dragged my tip across the length of her slit, watching her reaction. "You're sure?" I teased her clit with the head of my cock.

Shivering, she moaned and tilted her head back, her eyes closing. "Please," she whispered, sounding pained this time as her breathing grew heavier. "I need to feel you, all of you. Come inside me, Theo."

"Eyes. Give me your eyes." It's all I needed to say as I positioned myself at her entrance and began to push in until she took me to the hilt.

The woman panted, her eyes glazed over, her lips pursed, and her skin flushed. I couldn't begin to describe how she felt wrapped around me, and I had yet to move. Damn, she was tight, and I was terrified of humiliating myself like some horny teenager. I knew I wasn't small by any stretch of the imagination, and the slight tension in her brow told me that a little pain had come with the pleasure of my invasion. I waited, regaining my bearings, letting her adjust.

Nuzzling her nose, I pressed my lips to hers in a tender kiss. "Okay?"

"You feel amazing." Awe laced her words.

I chuckled. "I'll take that as a 'yes'." I pulled back and thrust in, and then I did it again, keeping things slow, savouring the silken feel of her heated depths, despite my desire to pound into her, find quick relief, and then rush to the next round. Had it been a decade ago, hell, even three years ago, that's what I'd have done. But this right here, with Morgan, was different. This moment of ours needed to be savored. *She* needed to be savored…worshipped.

When Morgan's hands squeezed my ass, I upped my tempo.

"Fuck, you feel so good," I growled, my face buried in the pillow next to her head, grinding my pelvis into hers.

"Oh, God! I'm going to come!"

"Not yet."

"Theo!"

"Wait for me, baby." I was so close. A few more thrusts would do it, and when it did, I cried out, "Now, baby! Let go!"

Her body stiffened and shook beneath me. She cried her release which I captured with my mouth, as I groaned mine into hers, feeling her core clamp down on me like a vice to the point I could barely move inside her.

Breathless, but refusing to allow any distance, I slid back and forth inside her, bringing us back down from our cloud of bliss. I kept from crushing her body with mine by leaning on my elbows, our mouths sharing the air, our faces were so close.

In a sudden manoeuvre, she tucked her head into my neck and hugged me tight before I heard her soft, "Two."

"Two what, baby?" I asked, rolling us over to our sides, careful to keep us connected.

"Orgasms," she mumbled against the skin of my chest.

My arms wrapped around her tight. I understood what she meant by that, and I was floored that as beautiful as she was, as forward as she could be, that she was bashful with certain aspects of sex, mainly talking about it.

"I hope that's not a complaint." I laughed, kissing the top of her head, and giving her another quick squeeze.

Her head lifted. Her eyes shimmered, and her lips quirked up. "No, I'm definitely not complaining." That quirking of her lips turned into what I could only describe as a devilish grin. Her hand roamed from my shoulder to stop and stroke my nipple before she brought her mouth to it to nip and then suckle. "My only complaint is that I have to wait until you're ready to go again."

CHAPTER 22

As I set to prove to Morgan that her waiting time was practically non-existent, reality set in that our escapade wasn't meant for a second round as a door slammed and a set of footsteps could be heard downstairs.

My lips froze on their descent to pay homage to Morgan's chest as I pulled back and stared at her, shock in equal measure.

"Auntie Morgan! Auntie Morgan!" a little voice yelled as little feet hit the stairwell.

Beneath me, panic took over Morgan's face. "Oh, fuck!" she said, and next thing I knew, she was shoving at my shoulders without much success at bucking me off. "Quick, get dressed!"

She didn't have to tell me twice, but before I could move, my body froze as I heard, "Auntie Morgan, where are you?" from the little one who wasn't very far from the bedroom we were in.

"I'll be right there, munchkin!" she shouted at the same time a woman called out, "Savi, get your tiny butt back down here, missy!" Little feet stopped and then proceeded closer.

My eyes played between the bedroom door and Morgan's wide gaze. "Who…what?" I sputtered.

"I'll tell you in a bit," Morgan whispered. "Just get off of me and cover up before–"

Just like the front door, the bedroom door slammed open and a little girl of about five or six stood in the entryway with her blonde pigtails, huffing and puffing for air through a few missing teeth. Before any of us could say anything, *Savi* beat us to the punch.

"Mommy, there's a man in Auntie Morgan's room and he's squishing her!" she squealed, another set of footsteps now making their way toward us in a hurried fashion.

My jaw dropped and then my body began to shake with laughter to which Morgan groaned and let her head fall back to the mattress while grumbling "Tattletale" to the little girl.

"I was just hugging her," I fibbed. It seemed like a plausible enough excuse for a child her age.

"Savannah, get out of there!" A woman came running in, coming to a dead halt behind the little girl as soon as her eyes met our compromising position. "Oh, God! Cover your eyes, baby, turn around, and go downstairs to the kitchen." A deep crimson suffused her face as she averted her eyes from us. "I'm so sorry, guys," she said in total mortification.

Instead of doing what she was told, the kid crossed her arms in a gesture of defiance, looked up at her mother and asked, "Mommy, why's that man hugging Auntie without his shirt on?"

Thank God for small reprieves in the form of bed sheets, which we'd crawled under shortly after our first round.

The woman's eyes bugged out of her head before she forced Savannah to turn away by the shoulders. "Kitchen, now!" she ordered, and when the child listened, she squeezed the bridge of her nose and sighed. "Hugging! If she only knew."

Morgan threw me under the bus. "Don't look at me, he's the one who gave her that idea."

"Hmm…right." She looked as if she was stifling a bout of giggles. "I'll be downstairs. Come find us when you're dressed. No 'hugging' until were gone, got it?"

"Kayla," Morgan began, "I'm–"

"Don't worry, Morgan," she started. "Savi had to learn about the birds and the bees some time, and since her father isn't around, she isn't going to learn it from me." She turned and left us.

As we dressed, my mind took a detour in its memory bank and snagged on the two names I'd just heard.

Fuck!

As realization hit, that I'd just come face-to-face with Damon's wife and child, my heartrate shot up. Blood rushed into my ears, my knees began to quake, and my stomach churned. My ass met the edge of the mattress when my knees gave out. I tried to massage the drumming pulse that beat at my temples, breathing to stave off the darkness hovering in my peripheral vision, threatening a total blackout. I was on the verge of a massive panic attack.

"Oh fuck," I mumbled.

Too busy with my turbulent emotions, trying to find my bearings, and dealing with reality, I barely noticed Morgan's approach.

"Theo?" I shook my head, my mouth dry as the Sahara. "Theo, talk to me. What's going on?" With much effort, she managed to pry my hands from my head and cradled my cheeks in her hands, effectively tilting my face so she could see it. "Shit."

"Yeah, that about sums it up."

"Theo—"

"That was Damon's woman," I croaked. "That's his…" I didn't finish. Instead, I led with, "They're all alone because of me."

"Theo, you know that isn't true," Morgan whispered, but her words could have been yelled and I wouldn't have heard them. Not the way she meant them.

I grabbed her wrists and pulled her hands away, setting her at a distance so I could stand. I ran a hand down my face and gulped. I knew this wasn't going to go over well but, "I've got to get out of here," came out before I could stop it.

Morgan blanched at my words. "What?"

"I can't, Morg."

"You keep saying that, and I've told–"

"Would you stop thinking about us for one damn second and take a good look at what just walked out of here!"

The woman flinched at my tone, but instead of backing down, she only looked more pissed off. "I've looked, Theo. I've been seeing for *years*! I've been there for them from the beginning, helped them, grieved with them, laughed with them, and–"

"So what?" I snorted. "You think they'll be just like you and open their arms and welcome me into the fold?"

"But–"

"I bet Kayla never expected that the guy you decided to entertain after your ex would end up–"

"Stop cutting me off!" she yelled back.

My rant continued as if she hadn't said anything, "getting your brother killed in the same mission, huh?"

"What?"

My head snapped to the bedroom door and found Kayla standing there, her eyes swimming with tears. There was no sign of little Savannah anywhere.

Thank the fucking Lord for small mercies!

Before the two women could say anything, I shoved my t-shirt over my head and made to leave the bedroom. When I got to Kayla's side, I forced my gaze to meet hers and whispered, "I'm sorry that you had to find out this way. He loved you so much," before I left.

My way downstairs was nothing but a blur, with the exception of the little girl that stood by the door as I paused to tie my work boots.

Her tiny hand touched my forearm. "Are you okay, mister?"

I knew I shouldn't have, but I looked at the tiny face that held her father's eyes and before I lost my cool, before I could even stop myself, I tilted the little one's head downward and kissed her hair. "I'm so sorry, shorty," I croaked before I straightened and fled Morgan's home.

I ran across the driveway and jumped in my truck, gunning the engine, and peeled out of there like my ass was on fire, and headed home.

CHAPTER 23

Slamming the front door after unlocking it, I dropped the keys to the floor and headed to the kitchen, pulling a beer out of the fridge. Popping the top, I downed half before moving toward the back door.

The back yard was slightly better than what the front had looked like before I had tamed it. The only thing that rendered it passable was the fact that I'd mowed part of the grass so it looked as if I had a yard.

I needed to get my anger and guilt out—to find something to purge the surge of emotions roiling through me.

The shed door listed to the side, one rusty hinge barely holding it in place as I pushed it open and grabbed the axe the previous owner had left behind. Maybe a little manual labour would be the ticket.

I lost count relatively quickly at how many logs I managed to split into firewood, but despite my tripling the size of the the pile, my emotions had yet to calm. So I moved on to destroying the dilapidated pergola that covered the patio.

With a large yank on the last rafter, I heard, "What are you doing?" which caused me to lose my footing and tumble the couple of feet off the stepladder to land on my ass with the piece of rotted wood over me.

"Jesus!" I shoved the scrap to the side, my heart beating wildly, and avoided the woman standing there by keeping my back to her. "You shouldn't be here," I growled.

The silence was heavy for a few seconds too long before a tiny whirlwind of a force ploughed into my side, wrapping her short arms around my neck.

I didn't move, too surprised to do so.

"Mommy says you knew my daddy?" Savannah stated more than asked.

I didn't answer.

"Mommy says you were brave just like him," the kid added, which still didn't garner a response from me.

"Savi," Kayla warned, coming into my line of sight.

"How come you came back but Daddy didn't?" Savannah questioned.

I shut my eyes and wished that I were anywhere else but right where I was. My answers weren't befitting of a child's ears.

"Savannah, that's enough!" Kayla said.

"You must have been the toughest of the bunch, right?" the little one persisted with a hint of awe to her voice. "That's what Auntie Morgan said."

I grunted as a response. *Tough…right.*

The little pipsqueak that refused to let go of me began to feel like a comfort and I found myself wrapping an arm around her and giving her a gentle squeeze.

Because I had yet to say anything, Savannah took it as a cue to keep rambling. "Why are you sad?"

Kayla gasped. "Savannah Morgan Smyth!"

But like always, Savannah ignored her mother's scolding. "You shouldn't be so sad," the child said, and I knew she was far from done, and sure enough, she didn't disappoint. "Did you know that Auntie Morgan has the bestest cure for when I'm sad?"

I snorted.

"It's true!" Savannah argued as if my reaction conveyed disbelief. "She gives the best hugs and she knows just where to tickle to make me laugh." Her giggle made my lips quirk.

"She doesn't tickle Mommy, but she does make her smile when she's feeling down. I don't like it when she's sad, so I help Auntie make Mommy feel better."

"I bet you're pretty good at it too," I mumbled. And she was good. Hell, I was beginning to feel the anger subside when nothing else I'd been doing had worked.

Savannah pulled back and gave me a look filled with conviction and a wide grin. "I'm the next bestest!" she announced.

I guffawed.

"See? It's working!" She turned to her mother. "Mommy, I told you I could do it!"

I snuck a quick look at Kayla. Her lips were in a firm line but her eyes shone with pride, clouded with reservation. When her eyes met mine, she mouthed, "I'm sorry."

I gave her a quick nod to let her know that it was fine.

"Savi, don't you think we should leave Mr. Lowell be?" she asked.

"Please, call me Theo," I said, as Savannah uttered a petulant "No!"

Morgan appeared around the house's corner. "I'm sorry, Kayla, our little shorty here snuck out on me while I was in the washroom. What's going on?" Her gaze travelled between Kayla and widened when she saw Savannah sitting across my lap and my arm around the little spitfire that took a lot after her aunt.

"We're making Theo happy again." Savannah grinned wide. "Well, *I'm* making him happy, but Mommy wants me to leave him alone."

Morgan's eyes met mine with hesitation. "Is it working?"

Savannah answered for me. "I think so. He laughed."

Morgan's lips quirked up and she arched a brow.

I shrugged my shoulders. "She's pretty good at it."

"Baby, we should get going," Kayla started.

"But you said you wanted to talk to him?" The little girl pouted.

That got my attention. "You did?" The woman nodded.

I looked over at Morgan, who's eyes softened. "It's time, Theo."

As anxious as I became, and as much as I knew it wasn't

going to be easy, something told me that she was right. It was time. Time for me to come clean with the wife of one of my best friends. Time for me to find forgiveness…to maybe purge the guilt that's been plaguing me since the mission that forever altered my life, that left me feeling undeserving…worthless.

Lifting Savannah off of me and setting her onto her feet, I got up, dusting myself off, and said, "Actually, Kayla, can I speak to you for a minute?"

CHAPTER 24

Morgan took Savannah back to her house as I escorted Kayla into my unfinished kitchen. I pulled a bottle of beer out for myself and said, "I know you're driving, so would you prefer some water or soda, I have lemonade too?"

Kayla paused from her perusal of my practically non-existent kitchen and mumbled, "Lemonade would be good."

Now that it was just her and I, my nerves were getting the better of me. I stalled the inevitable conversation I had instigated by topping a tall glass with ice and grabbing the pitcher of the tart juice from the fridge.

Pouring slowly, Kayla picked up on my delaying tactic and said, "I need to know what happened."

My shoulders slouched, my resolve deflated a little, but this was it. This was the time to find out if she would see me as the killer I imagine myself to be, or the broken man that Morgan saw.

I gestured to one of the two chairs that currently served as my kitchen set and Kayla took a seat while I put her glass of lemonade in front of her. I took the other seat and gulped down a hefty sip of my beer before setting it down and studying the woman that sat across from me.

She was young, beautiful, strong, whether she was willing to admit it or not, and a good woman, from what I remembered Damon saying.

Before Kayla could commence with her questions, I spoke. And I didn't stop, even going as far as to recount what I'd gone through with my capture, and how I got back.

"I always knew that I'd end up a widow," Kayla whispered when I finished telling her the tale that had killed more than just my teammates. It had killed long-wished-for dreams as well. Theirs, hers, Savannah's, Morgan's…mine too, if I were being entirely honest.

"Kayla–"

She cut me off. "Steve loved the marines. Aside from being a father and spending his life with me, being a marine was his life, it was who he was. I know you believed that at one point too." I nodded. I had. Kayla's hand crossed the table and cool fingers landed over my forearm. "God, the things you've been through."

"I don't need anyone's pity," I mumbled, retracting my arm from her touch. "I told you the story so you would know the truth, not the romanticized version they most likely told you. Smyth was under my command. He was following orders and he died doing that. It's my fault and I take the blame."

I got a less than enthused, "Wow," from the woman, which made my head snap up and my eyes move to hers. "You really are the self-sacrificing son of a bitch Steve talked about."

"Excuse me?"

"Theo, we've never met until today, but I know you. Aside from Morgan coming to me and telling me she'd met you on the weekend after my husband's birthday, you need to know that Steve wrote and talked to me about you. He said that you're a good man, one who would do anything for the ones you care about." My response came in the way of a curt nod. "You'd give it all away, wouldn't you…your happiness, your family, your friends, your life? You would have given it all up if it meant that they'd lived."

"And what's wrong with that?"

"What's wrong?" She shot up to her feet, agitated beyond what I expected. "You have the gall to ask me what's wrong?"

"Yeah."

"What's wrong is that *my* man didn't die so you'd be miserable. He didn't die because he was under you. He didn't die because you told him to drive over that fucking roadside bomb. And he sure as hell didn't die to have you get captured, tortured and used against and by our government, Sergeant Lowell! He was ready to die to give us all a better life just like you were, so you telling me that you'd die just so he could come back, though honorable as some would say it is, only tarnishes my husband's sacrifice."

Just like Morgan calling me by my nickname, Kayla calling me by my title made me sit up straighter. No one had called me that since the day I'd received my discharge papers. I don't even recall the last time someone had spoken to me that way except for my superiors. And the woman was on a roll, but this time, her voice grew softer.

"Can't you see? You've already died before even leaving this life. That's not what he—*no*—what *you* fought for. You're no hero, Lowell, but you sure as hell did what so many of us couldn't. Some don't understand, but having a father in the Marines, and his fathers before him being part of the same brotherhood, helps me understand. There's no fucking glory in what you do. The pats on the back don't mean shit. I know that! What means something is that you stood up when others couldn't…when they wouldn't. You fought for your friends and family. You came back! You–"

"Kayla, listen–"

"No, *you* listen!" She stomped her foot. "You've got something special right here. Morgan told me about you before today, but it wasn't all about how you knew Steve."

She did?

"Yes, she did," she said as if reading my mind. "She cares a lot more than you think. She's moving on from the loss of her brother, just like I am, just like Savannah is. But you haven't at all, have you, Theo? You walk around, carrying the weight of the dead, fearing that letting them go means that you once again failed them."

"I suppose that maybe you're right," I mumbled.

"You know I am." Her face bore a look of confidence in her deduction. "So what you have to ask yourself is, are you ready to come back to the land of the living?"

Hmm. Was I ready to do that?

"Are you ready, Sergeant Lowell?" she asked again. "Instead of living like the dead because they can't, can you try and live a life that's worth something to be proud of, something that Steve Damon Smyth could be proud of? Can you live a life that rivals any that the men and women you lost would be happy seeing you living?"

I cleared my throat and met her eyes with mine, but my voice came out with a croak and filled with emotion, "You're not the first to tell me this, Kayla."

"And I'm not going to be the last." The woman crossed her arms over her chest, sat down, and gave me the stubborn look that was all too familiar.

Oh yeah, Savannah didn't just have her father's looks and her aunt's attitude. It seemed that the stubbornness ran on both sides of the family, because her mother had more than enough of it in her pinky finger.

I nodded in assent. "Seems that everyone around me has been telling me the same thing since I've come back."

"That's because we're right."

"Maybe you are," I said for the first time, leaving myself open to the fact that I wasn't to blame for what happened over there.

"And how does that make you feel?"

I scrunched up my nose at her. "What are you, a shrink?"

"Among other things." She shrugged her shoulders. "After what I say next, I think you'll have to ask yourself a very important question. If you can answer 'yes' to that question, then I'd have to say you're off to a very good start."

"And what's that?"

"Theo, I know there is one thing that you haven't heard from me yet that you need to, but you'll never admit it."

"There is?"

"Stop playing dumb, it's unbecoming." She smirked and

her face straightened to complete seriousness. "I forgive you."

Damn, were all women this confusing? "But you said I didn't do anything."

"It doesn't matter if you did or didn't. You believe you did, so I forgive you," she paused. "The question is can you forgive yourself?"

"But I didn't do anything."

"Now I think we're getting somewhere." Her eyes twinkled, but her lips remained in a firm line. "So you forgive yourself?"

Leaning forward, staring down at the table with my hands in my hair, I thought about that for a moment. Logically, I knew everything that happened had been out of my hands. Psychologically, I felt I had failed, as if there was more I could have done. Could I really forgive myself for that? What's more, could I move on and give myself the life I knew my men would have had, honoring them as I did?

"The short answer should be 'yes'," I said. "The long answer is that it's a hell of a lot more complicated, but I think I can learn to."

"Good. That's all I want to hear." With that, Kayla got to her feet again and proceeded to walk toward the back door, while I watched on. As she reached the exit to the kitchen, she looked at me over her shoulder. "Take care of her. She's my sister in every sense but blood, and I'll cut your dick off with a dull, rusty Ka-bar if you ever hurt her, you hear?" And then she was gone.

CHAPTER 25

Kayla's words played over and over in my head.

Could I forgive myself?

Well wasn't that the crux of it all!

Sitting at the table as I pondered this, I realized I was no longer alone when soft hands ran over my back to pause onto my shoulders with a light squeeze. Morgan didn't need to speak for me to know it was her.

"You shouldn't be here. Not after the way I spoke to you."

"You can't get rid of me that easily, Theo."

"So it seems. You should be running in the other direction. You've had more than enough to deal with for a lifetime."

"I'm a big girl."

"I think I get it." I grabbed her hand and held it, pushing my chair back and pulling her so she sat on my lap. She studied my face, grasping each side with her hands in a tender manner before leaning in and pressing her forehead against mine. "I just don't know if I can do it," I whispered against her lips.

"We'll take it one day at a time. Now that you know that there's no forgiveness to be given but your own, we can work on that. Just don't push those who care about you away when you're more deserving than any of us to be happy again."

"I want to be happy." My lips grazed hers.

"Then I promise I'll try to make that happen, baby." And she sealed her vow with a light press of her mouth to mine.

"You make it easier." I pulled her in tight against me, causing her to wrap her arms around my shoulders as I clamped my mouth to hers, a hand of mine finding the back of her head, holding her in place as I set to devouring her mouth in an intense kiss that showed her how much she affected me.

The place was quiet, the rain pinged at the windowpanes, loaning to the feel that we were the only ones in the world. I had Morgan cradled against me, her head on my shoulder with the knit throw covering our nakedness on the couch. It was a little piece of heaven.

Morgan's hand ran up my chest, her fingers playing over the tattoo that lay between my pecks, climbing over my collarbones. She sighed.

"That sounded loaded," I remarked.

"Not at all." She lifted her head and kissed my chin. "I was just thinking about how it's been one hell of a day. I know I should go home, but–"

"Don't go." It sounded like a plea even to my ears. "I mean, you can stay, I want you here."

"With the way you left, Kayla going after you, and then Savi leaving so I ended up chasing her here, I never had time to lock the house up. I have to go and–"

I kissed her before she could finish. "It's okay."

"Come with me." Her eyes displayed guarded hope that I would and my mouth ran dry, unsure of what my next move should be. "I promise I won't hit you with another two-by-four. I'm really sorry about that, by the way."

I laughed easily as I pressed my lips to her forehead. "Are you sure?" My eyes studied her face for any note of doubt to her invitation. "I might never leave."

She kissed the left side of my chest. "Would that be so bad?"

"I thought you said you weren't looking for forever?" I said, bemused.

"It's not." Her eyes sparkled and she smirked. "It's right now." She climbed over me, straddling my hips, her hands on either side of my head and leaned forward. "No one knows where we'll be tomorrow, a year, or twenty from now, Theo."

My hands roamed over her thighs, up to her sides, my thumbs rubbing just below her ample breasts. "Yeah, but we've got a small problem, Morg." She recoiled at that, sat up and stared down at me. When she made to get off of me, I grabbed her hips and pulled her back down, grinding my pelvis into hers. Her eyes glazed over. I lifted my hand up and tucked a few loose strands of her hair behind her ear. "Oh yes, a little problem."

"And what's that?" Morgan's hands were braced on my stomach.

I grabbed her wrists, pulled her down towards me and with a swift twist of my hips, I managed to flip us so she lay on her back under me, and I nuzzled at her ear before whispering the next. "What if I end up wanting forever?"

CHAPTER 26

Finding a soft warm body pressed against mine the next morning, and every morning for a week afterward, was new for me. Morgan's tight ass pressed into my crotch certainly did things for my libido, and as each day passed, I became increasingly aware of how happy a simple thing as having someone to wake up to made me.

Much to my regret, I left Morgan's sleep-warmed form, headed for the bathroom to take care of business, then made my way to the kitchen, hitting the percolator's *on* button on my way to the fridge.

Once fed, I headed out to check on things and greet the crew of guys that would be showing up to finish the outside component of Morgan's upstairs addition today. It wasn't until I'd entered the old barn I'd been storing some tools and equipment in that I knew something was up.

What the fuck?

My temper was still at its edge as I neared Morgan's driveway with more provisions from the hardware store, to replace the damaged items I'd found in her barn this morning. I'd spoken with my workers only to get nowhere. No one knew anything, and no one tipped my radar as guilty either.

The hairs on the back of my neck stood on end as I checked my rearview mirror. Something didn't feel right when I spotted an older red Ford pickup truck, which had been behind me since my hitting the outskirts of town.

As I turned to pull up Morgan's driveway, the tanker in question—which had slowed down—sped up and drove past the turnoff and kept going before I could get a license plate number or attempt at recognizing the driver.

I shook away the sensation that something was off and exited my truck, reaching for the couple of bags that lay on the seat beside me, and headed for the tailgate to get the rest. Collecting the gallons of paint, I headed for the front door.

"Morg," I called out. "I'm back!"

With the music cranked up, I knew exactly where she was. With how high the decibels to her music was, it was a wonder that this woman wasn't anywhere near deaf. Hearing her voice above the country tune she had on made me smile. She may have nothing on Brantley Gilbert, but she sure as hell knew how to *kick it in the sticks* as the song coined with the same name said it.

When I opened the room door, all thoughts of continuing with the day's project or the suspicious tail I had acquired on my way home vanished.

With her hips swinging, hair tucked in some loose messy bun, her skin coated with a light sheen of sweat, a roller in her hand and paint spatter all over her arms, Morgan had never looked any better.

And then she did this little shimmy manoeuvre with her hips that set my blood on fire. I wanted her, and I wanted her like yesterday.

Fuck it!

Setting everything on the floor, I couldn't help myself. I snuck up on her, grabbed her hips and pulled her abruptly to bump her rear to my front.

"Holy shit!" The roller went flying as she spun around, then sucker punched me in the shoulder. "You ass, you scared me half to death!"

I grinned down at her, then kissed her forehead. "I'm sorry, but this little sprite had me mesmerized, and I couldn't very well let her go on with her hypnotizing dance now could I?" I kissed her now smiling lips as my arms squeezed her to me. "Now what was that last move you did?"

"Hmm…" she murmured against my lips as I broke away from hers. "You mean this one?"

She turned in my arms and proceeded to rub up against my front like a cat in heat. Yeah, that was the one. I groaned.

With the desk only a few feet away, I nudged Morgan's hips forward until her balance was thrown and she had to lean forward onto the sturdy piece of wooden furniture to maintain her footing.

"Theo!"

"Don't move," I instructed her, my hands running up the side of her thighs to cup her ass. "Seeing this ass in these shorts all day has been driving me crazy." She moaned when my thumb rubbed against the seam of the jean material that ran over the crease between her legs. The heat radiating from her along with her distinctive scent of arousal had me salivating.

"W-what are you doing?" Morgan asked when my hands reached around her to undo the button of her shorts. "We have people floating around the house, you can't–"

"Baby, the only work they're doing is outside today." I rubbed my crotch against her delectable bottom. "If they need anything, they know to knock or ring the doorbell."

"But–"

"Shh." I nipped her earlobe. Her body quivered against mine and with a few quick flicks of my wrist, Morgan's shorts were on their way down along with her underwear. "I want to thank you for the show. In fact…" I reached to unzip and take myself out of my jeans, rubbing the tip of my cock in the slickened crease between her legs with one hand while I kept her pressed against me with the other. "I feel hard-pressed to be thankful in a very thorough manner."

As if knowing what I wanted her to do next, Morgan spread her legs to allow me more room to move between her thighs.

Lining myself up with her heat, I slowly entered her, hissing "Yes." She whimpered as I invaded her depths, melting into me. "So sweet, so hot, so slick." I licked my lips. "I love how wet you get for me."

"Just for you," Morgan purred as I began to pull out.

"For me," I said and thrust forward.

"Yes! You!"

Her declaration did something to me.

"Brace yourself, baby, you're in for one hell of a ride," I announced right before I pulled back and slammed in as far as I could go.

Morgan cried out as her hands braced on the edge of the desk and I set the rhythm.

There wasn't anything soft about the way I brought us pleasure. It wasn't sex. It was hot. It was sweaty. It was pure carnal rapture—animalistic fucking at its finest.

Hard. Rough. Loud.

The minute Morgan's climax took her, I felt her insides clench down on me like a vice and I was a goner. "That's it, baby. Take it all," I said, spilling myself inside her depths, bringing forth a long keening cry from her as her pussy clenched me even harder as a second wave of orgasmic bliss rose on the tails of her first.

We collapsed to the desk where I was careful not to crush Morgan. Our breathing stabilized, and when I could think straight enough, I pulled out of her and flipped her so she could face me. The look of pure satisfaction on the woman's face was something to boast about.

"Sweetheart?" I asked through the smirk that had over-taken my face.

"That was…" She raised her head and gave me a hard kiss before collapsing onto the desk, her chest rising and dropping rapidly. "Just, wow!"

The reality of her size sunk in. "I wasn't too rough?"

She shook her head, a grin spreading across her face. "Baby, I might be small, but I'm not made out of glass." Her hand came up and cupped my cheek. I turned my head and kissed her palm without losing contact with her eyes. "I loved it, but I have a question."

"What's that?"

"Where the hell did that come from, and when can we do it again?"

CHAPTER 27

Nearly two weeks had gone by, and I wish I could say that the odd break-and-enter episode in Morgan's barn had been a one-time occurrence, but it wasn't the case. After yesterday's setback, however, I knew that someone was trying to send us a message.

Finding thousands of dollars' worth of my equipment not only damaged, but some of it ruined beyond repair, was more than enough for me to bring in the police.

They came.

They investigated.

They left with nothing more than a report for their files and a half-empty reassurance that they were investigating things and that it was most likely teenagers. Much to my annoyance, but feeling the need to spare Morgan any more grief and financial worry, I had my men help move the tools, equipment, and the shipments of building materials onto my property, locking them away in my garage, and only bringing them along when we needed them.

Two days later, I got up early to start on Morgan's kitchen flooring.

As I walked to her garage—and not her barn—to fetch the tile we'd just locked up there the night before to make today's task a bit easier on us, I knew something was wrong when I found the padlock clean cut and lying on the ground with the door ajar.

Sonofabitch!

Pushing the door open further to peek inside, I took in the mess I knew awaited me.

In heaps of rubble lay most of Morgan's new Italian slate tile. Cans of paint, varnish, caulking—whatever liquid that could be found—were splattered from wall to wall, floor to ceiling. In the middle of the messy deluge was Damon's classic '69 Charger that—according to what Morgan had told me a few weeks back—he'd finished restoring right before his last deployment.

I took one last gander at the piles of what could mostly be considered garbage, and resigned myself to a day of dealing with the calls to my insurance and the cops for the second time in as many days, as I headed back to the house.

"What's wrong?" Morgan asked as I walked into the kitchen, my face clearly displaying my anger. She was barefoot, dressed in nothing but a loose fitting t-shirt that hung off her shoulder, holding a cup of steaming coffee out to me. I took it from her at the same time she said, "It happened again, didn't it?"

I nodded. "It's worse."

"What about–"

Before I could shake my head or say anything else, Morgan rushed out of the house and toward the garage. Setting my coffee mug down, I rushed after her. I caught up with her just as she stormed through the garage door.

I knew what she was looking for.

With a pained cry, she dropped to her knees as the sight of her brother's hard work showed its ruined state.

"Baby." I tried to get her to stand, but she was limp, covering her face with her hands as she sobbed. I crouched down and wrapped my arms around her. "Morgan." I turned her face into my chest and cradled her head against me.

"It's all I had left." She sniffled. "This junker he loved so much, and this house. Except now, it's really junk."

"It's fixable, baby," I attempted to console her. "I'll take care of it." Keeping an arm wrapped around her back, I reached under her knees to pick her up. Her bloodied knees made me wince. Morgan's body shook with sobs as she wrapped her arms around my neck and held onto me. "Let's get you cleaned up and then I'll call the police."

After the last incident, Paxton had asked me why I hadn't contacted my old friend Shane. Well, I guess I was going to now. This wasn't a sporadic innocent act of bored delinquency. This was someone after my livelihood, and they were choosing to pick their fight with me on my woman's turf. The lingering question was why was this happening.

CHAPTER 28

Opening the front door, I was met with a grin I could never forget.

"Well if it isn't Sergeant Theodore Lowell!" I moved to the side to let Detective Shane Peters in, shaking his offered hand.

"Peters, how the hell are you, man?"

"Better than you, it seems," he said, his eyes snagging on Morgan who stood behind me. "And I take it this is your girl?"

Morgan moved forward and introduced herself, albeit a little withdrawn.

"Sweetheart," I turned Morgan around and guided her toward the sofa, "why don't you tell Shane here your side of everything and then maybe you can go lie down for a bit."

Dejected, she nodded and in a very robotic fashion, she proceeded to explain what's been going on. When she finished, I excused us and guided her upstairs, made sure she was comfortable, and assured her that I'd be back soon.

As my feet hit the landing, Shane grinned. "I like her."

I chuckled. "It's impossible not to. Believe me, I tried."

My friend's demeanor changed to one so serious. "Now that your girl is out of earshot, why don't you tell me why these disturbances seem to be targeting you?"

I pondered his words for a few seconds and came back with, "Your guess is as good as mine."

"You just got back into town after being away for the last ten years."

"How does that have anything to do with what's going on?" My frustration was growing, and by what Peters said next, it was evident that the detective could sense it.

"Listen, T, someone's got a beef with you and your woman. It's my job to stop them, but until you start answering my questions—"

"With all due respect, Shane, I grew up here. Hell, you were there back in the day. I'm sure some people aren't happy to see me back in town. It's not like I was known to keep my nose clean. People around here have long memories." I sighed, running a hand down my face. "You want to know who I think it is, I'm telling you that I don't know. I haven't talked to anyone other than the crew of guys I brought in to fix Morgan's house, my brother's lawyer friend, and my own family, unless you're thinking old man Saunders at the hardware store on Picket is behind this."

The man's lips quirked on one side, clearly remembering the shenanigans we used to get up to. "Fine," Shane said. "I get it. You've been quiet."

"Yeah. I'm not proud of the shit I pulled when I was a kid, but that's just it, I was a kid. Hell, I was bad enough for my parents to ship off to military school. Why would anyone look down at me when you were just as bad, and look at you now."

Shane grinned. "Hard to believe, huh?"

"Nah, I always knew you'd end up just like your old man."

"You were gone for a hell of a long time," he said. "What was it that you did, exactly?"

"I know you're asking about everything I've been up to in the last three years, but aside from telling you that I've seen the worst of what the world has to offer," I crossed my arms and sported a wry smile, "the rest is confidential."

"They told us you were dead." The sad look on my old friend's face struck a nerve.

"What's this got to do with—"

"Do you think that maybe someone that you might have worked with–"

It was my turn to cut the man off. "Anyone I worked with is dead. I lost my team in my last mission, Shane."

The man didn't look at all surprised at what I divulged, more sympathetic really. "I know." He leafed through his notepad. "But that was three years ago. Surely this confidential bullshit of yours has something to do with other missions, no?"

"Yeah, there were other missions."

"Is it possible that– I mean, you yourself said you've seen the worst of what the world has to offer. Clearly you've dealt with–"

A dry laugh escaped my lips. "I've worked alone over the last three years, Shane. I've met my fair share of shady people in that time. Some I've had to side with at one point or another in order to get what I needed from them. I'm not saying more, but the likelihood of them knowing anything about me and my personal life, not to mention to come after me when I'm no longer active, is ridiculous."

"I know, but I have to cover all my bases, and let's face it, if you double-crossed someone, depending on their state of mind, I wouldn't completely dismiss them." The man paused to look at me and shook his head with what looked like disbelief. "Damn, but it's really good to see you, T."

"Yeah, I wish it were under better circumstances."

"Some of the guys and me get together for a few drinks and a round of pool every couple of weekends," he said. "You might want to show up at McAskill's on Friday. It sure would be good to catch up."

I nodded. "You buying?"

"The least I can do to reintroduce you to the fold, seeing as you made it back from the sandbox after a decade," he said. "Fucking pretty boy. It disgusts me how that scar across your eyebrow hasn't done you a disservice in the looks department."

Chuckling, I gave him a punch to the shoulder. "I'll be there."

"Good." Shane's eyes went to the stairwell leading to the upstairs bedrooms. "Not sure what's going on here, but do me a favor and call me if anything else pops up, all right?" He pulled out a business card from his lapel pocket and started for the door. "And by the way, didn't you know you weren't supposed to dip your wick in the client pool?"

"Fuck off." The man harrumphed as I flipped him off. "She's more than a client and you know it."

The man's face took a sorrowful look that had me wondering what it was that I'd said that had caused it. "I know," he said, his voice soft. "Keep an eye on her, the way she looked before she went up there tells me that she may be close to her breaking point. I'll see you around, T. McAskill's. Friday. At seven."

Without waiting for a reply from me, he exited the house.

Having missed lunch, I headed into Morgan's kitchen to see what kind of food I could put together for us. I made us a few sandwiches, grabbed a bag of chips, a couple of bottles of water, and washed up some berries.

Morgan was still sound asleep when I let myself into her bedroom.

Setting the tray of food down on her bedside table, I couldn't help but take in the sleeping beauty before me.

So innocent, yet so naughty.

Peaceful, yet a riot at the best of times.

Precious and frail, yet the strongest person I had ever known, because her strengths were all from within.

Before I could wake her, Morgan's eyes opened and met mine.

"Hey…" I tucked a few stray strands of her hair behind her ear. "How are you feeling?"

She groaned. "Like I'm living a nightmare." I gave her a sympathetic look. "What did Shane say?"

"He thinks it's got something to do with me."

"What?" She bolted, seated upright in bed. "But that's ridiculous!"

"No, it's not, really," I told her.

"What else did he say?"

Lifting the tray of food, I set it down between us and smirked. "How about we eat and I tell you what Shane thinks, and then what he said about you." I leaned over and kissed the confused look on her face.

CHAPTER 29

Friday came around and I found myself walking into McAskill's shortly after seven, despite my reluctance to leave Morgan alone. Tonight was the first evening she and I would spend apart since we'd gotten together, even though we'd never put a label on what we were. Being in our thirties, it seemed odd to call her my girlfriend, but I suppose that's what she was.

There hadn't been any new developments with the investigation on the happenings at her house, nor had anything new occurred throughout the rest of the week.

"Well, look who's back from the dead!"

"Kippers!" My jaw dropped at the sight of the man. "Since when have you been back stateside?"

The man got up and that's when reality hit. The limp said more than enough when he took the few steps to meet up with me, grasping my fist and pulling me in for a rough pat on the back. "It's good to have you back, brother," he said. "I knew they couldn't break you."

If anyone could remotely understand the nature of what I'd been through during my deployments, it was Dalton Kippers. Despite suffering his own version of hell, to see the man standing before me made me feel more at home, less of an outcast, if you will. Then again, so did the sight of the other three men who stood behind him.

"If I didn't know that Peters was telling the truth, I'd say the poster boy for our armed forces has just walked through the door." That baby face might have been able to fool all the ladies back in the day, but his mouth would always get him in trouble. There was no mistaking that the idiot who'd just spoken was none other than Brycen Mathews.

"Well if it isn't Baby-Face." Dalton moved aside to let me shake hands with Brycen. "Cade Harwick," I said as I set my eyes on the next man in line. Where Brycen was slighter than the rest of us, Cade was the largest—not only in height, but muscle too.

Cade grabbed me by the back of the neck and pulled me in for a man-hug of his own. "It's damn good to see you, man," he said. "I should have known they were full of shit when I got the news."

I pulled back and looked at the four men that stood in front of me. Right there was a piece of history that made me feel connected to the world again. Alive. It was a piece of me that I hadn't realized had gone missing over the years, until now.

And as if a decade had never gone by, the camaraderie resumed.

It was eleven when Shane's cell rang.

"Don't do it, man," Cade told him, shaking his head. "It's your first night off in two weeks."

Shane's eyes looked confused then met mine before he said, "I have to get this," and walked toward the exit.

Call it a sixth sense, but something told me that I was involved in whatever conversation he was about to have.

Within five minutes, as I was bent to take a shot at the pool table, Peters was back asking me where my phone was.

"Why?" I asked as I pulled it out of my pocket only to realize that I'd forgotten to charge the thing and it was dead.

"She tried to call you but couldn't get through. Something's going on at Morgan's."

"Fuck!" I threw the cue onto the table's felt, knocking around the few balls that were still in play. "We've got to go."

"Who's Morgan?" Cade asked from behind me.

"His woman," Shane answered before I could.

"It's just like you," Brycen jumped in. "You're back for like, what, five minutes, and you're already getting some ass."

"Bryce," Dalton shook his head in warning, having already read the tick in my jaw for the sign that it was.

"He's right, Brycen," Shane said. "You don't want to go there with this one."

My blood was boiling. Morgan needed me and I hadn't been available when she tried to reach me.

I should have been there to protect her. Deciding against chastising myself about it, or explaining myself to the men, I started toward the door, saying, "I'll catch you guys later. I'm heading out."

Twenty-five minutes later, I pulled up the drivewayto find complete chaos. The visual I took in was haunting. Beyond the white and blue flashing over the property, I noticed an open front door, broken windows and slander—what I could only assume was spray-painted—across the front walls to the house.

What made it worse was the sight of Morgan, wrapped in a blanket, sitting on her front porch steps all alone. Police and CSI wandered about, walking in and out of the house, paying her no mind.

I rushed to the woman who sported such a look of defeat and pale demeanour that I couldn't help myself. I pulled her up to her feet and crushed her to my chest. "Baby, I'm so sorry," I whispered against her hair.

Clutching me like a lifeline, her body shook like a leaf. As I rubbed up and down her back, I could feel the tension in her shoulders easing.

Pulling back, I cupped the sides of her face in both of my hands. "Morg, what happened?"

"I fell asleep on the couch and woke up to the windows being smashed," she explained. "I-I didn't think." She bit her lip. "I was caught off guard, and I rushed out of the house without thinking."

"What?" My hands grabbed onto her upper arms, squeezing a bit harder than I should have, if the subtle wince-like look on her face was anything to go by. I released my grip immediately, rubbing away the discomfort I'd caused. "Baby, you could have been hurt."

"I know that. But when I opened the door, I saw this older red Ford pickup truck driving off from the end of the driveway. By then, it was too late. When I ran to the living room to get my phone and call you, that's when I saw this mess." Her arm waved toward the graffiti that graced the house behind her.

"Thank God you're okay." I pulled her into me once more. Just as I was about to tell her that I didn't know what I would do without her, tires on gravel skidding to a halt nearby had me turning us so I could see who it was that had arrived.

"T!" Paxton came running at us, Alissa following close on his heels.

"What are you doing here?" I asked.

"I called them," Morgan mumbled into my chest.

My head snapped downward to look at the top of her head. "You did?"

She nodded before meeting my gaze. "I couldn't get a hold of you after I called the cops, so I called Allie, and then Shane from the business card you left on the fridge."

"You can't sleep here tonight," Alissa said as she took in the state of the house. "It's not safe."

"You're right," I said and studied the woman who had managed to worm her way into my heart, and steal it. "You're coming home with me."

"Theo," she started, but I cut her off.

"It's not up for debate." I kissed her mouth hard as it opened in protest once more. "No arguments, Morgan. You damn well nearly gave me a heart attack tonight."

It took some work, but Morgan and I managed to convince my brother and his wife to head back to Jake and Danica's where they'd left the kids before heading over. Not only did I want Morgan and I to be alone, but with the attacks escalating, I wasn't willing to put my brother and his family at risk unless it was absolutely necessary. It was bad enough that Morgan was suffering through any of this at all, but since she was alone, I had appointed myself as her protector.

No sooner had we arrived to my house, I dropped Morgan's bag by the front door, did up the deadbolt and turned the woman so her back was up against the wall.

"How are you feeling?" I pressed my body against hers, cradling the side of her face with one hand as the other braced me from applying my whole weight on her.

"Exhausted, but wired. It's hard to explain."

"It's the adrenaline from everything that's going on. That exhaustion you feel right now will feel ten times worse when the adrenaline surge wears off." The pad of my thumb skimmed her bottom lip, her tongue slipping out to lick the tip of it, causing my body to heat up. "Baby," I groaned.

"I need you, Theo," she whispered.

"You have me." I covered her lips with a soft peck. "You'll always have me." I repeated the soft brush of my lips against hers. "Now let's get you to bed."

"I don't think I can sleep," she confessed as I grabbed her bag in one hand, her hand in the other, and pulled her toward the stairs. "I can't take my mind off of what's been happening. Why is this happening, Theo?"

My silence was held until we'd reached my bedroom. It was the only room that had been relatively whole and liveable when I'd bought the property. Depositing her bag by the dresser, I went to Morgan who stood by the side of the bed.

Pushing her down so she sat on it, I kneeled in front of her. "I don't know why this is going on, but we'll get through this." With her face in my hands once more, I bent it down and kissed her forehead before pulling away enough to look into her eyes, and with potent resolve, I repeated myself. "I promise we *will* get through this. Together."

Her eyes closed as she let my words sink in. "Together," she whispered before glassy eyes met mine and she leaned in with a feral kiss.

Her arms came around my neck as she held me to her, causing me to lean up, my arms bracing me on either side of her thighs. Morgan's lips left mine, trailing nips and licks down my chin, to my neck and back up to my mouth where she paused to look me in the eyes. "Make love to me, Theo. Make me forget. I need a hero for tonight."

I groaned. "Baby, I'm no–"

Cool fingers covered my mouth, ceasing my words. "Tonight you are, in my eyes." Her words were filled with so much sincerity that she had me believing her, though it couldn't have been further from the truth in my mind.

Even though I had decided I wasn't going to argue with her, "But I wasn't there," was out before I could stop it.

She cupped my face in her hands. "You were there eventually. That's what counts."

"But I was late and anything could have happened to you." My voice shook with so much pent up emotion, the most prominent being the sense of loss I felt tugging at my heart at the thought of never being able to be with her again.

"Nothing did, baby," she said. "And you showed up regardless."

"But–"

She sighed. "No more, Theo. I'm not going to let the man I love tear himself to pieces over this."

My breath seized in my lungs, my heart leapt. "Say that again?"

Morgan's eyes twinkled as her hands held my face firmly. "Theo Lowell, I love you."

I savoured her words with my eyes closed for a split second.

Before I knew it, Morgan was on her back, my body covering hers, her wrists restrained on either side of her head by my hands as I looked down at her. "Tell me I'm dreaming," I whispered against her ear and pulled back to look at her face. "Tell me that it was the heat of the moment, or because of crazy emotions, because a woman like you can't possibly love a man like me."

"Well, if this is a dream, I don't ever want to wake up." She smiled for the first time since before I'd left her for my guys' night. "And I guess I've achieved the impossible then, Theo, because I do love you. You might think you've failed or that you'll never be good enough, but all of that is keeping you from seeing the man you really are."

"Morg." Fuck, she undid me. "I–"

"I love you," she repeated, and even though it was the fourth time in as many minutes, it still felt as good, if not better, than the first time. "That's the whole of it. It's my decision and the best damn one I've ever made in my life."

A laugh bubbled out of me and I attacked her lips with mine briefly before I pulled away and buried my face in her hair, taking this new reality of ours in. As I pulled away, I found myself unable to hide from her anymore. "God help me, but I'm feeling selfish." I gave her a hard peck.

She harrumphed. "And so you should feel entitled to be."

"I love you too, Morgan Smyth. I think I've loved you since you first called me up and asked me to plug up your hole." Her blush had me laughing. "Then again, it might have been the drenched clothing that was plastered to your body when you answered your door that first day. I had the hardest time focusing…"

Her eyes narrowed as she tried to free her

wrists from my grip. "You men are all the same, aren't you?"

"Hmm." I nuzzled her nose before staring into her eyes. "Honestly, I think I fell in love with you the minute you refused to let me walk away."

Morgan's face lost its playful look and her features softened. "Really?"

I nodded. "Here was this tiny spitfire of a woman with a larger-than-life attitude, telling me how things were going to go. Morg, I've gotten used to fighting all my life. I fought in school to be the best at sports because fighting for my grades didn't prove anything. I fought my brother for girls, my dad because I could never seem to please him." Her head bobbed up and down, urging me to continue. "I fought to get through basic training, the sandbox, through being a prisoner…torture." My eyes burned and my throat closed up. "Dammit, I fought just to stay alive even though I'd lost everyone…everything I knew. And then there's you." I took a deep breath, trying to calm my roiling emotions. "Baby, I fought my feelings, I fought *you*. Don't you see?"

"See what, Theo?"

"Out of all of this fighting, all I've ever had was someone fighting with or against me."

"Theo…" Morgan's voice cracked.

"But I've never had someone go to *war* for me, to fight *for* me." Morgan's breath whooshed out. "That's what makes you different from everyone else. I know my family and friends love me. Hell, I love them too. But you, you top them by miles, Morgan. You win my heart, my soul…me."

Silent tears began to fall down her face and I let go of her wrists to wipe at them. "I never wanted to go to war, Morgan, but for you, I'd start one, or however many it will take, if it means me spending the rest of my days with you, making you happy, seeing you smile, coming home to you and–"

"Baby," she said through the stream of tears leaking from her beautiful eyes.

"I'm serious, Morgan Smyth." I kissed a tear-stained

cheek. "I want it all with you." I kissed the other. "Forever." I aimed for her lips.

Words ceased because at that point our bodies spoke volumes larger than our voices ever could.

CHAPTER 31

Like every other morning that followed a night spent with Morgan, I awoke to find myself wrapped around her back, my arms surrounding her while she slept.

As I shifted slightly, Morgan sighed peacefully, a perfect indicator that she was waking.

"I love you," I whispered into her ear before kissing it, the hand covering her stomach, slowly gliding over her soft, heated skin, down toward her folds, which had remained bare—as with the rest of our bodies—from last night's frivolities.

Sliding a finger through her damp folds generated a whimpering moan from Morgan. With a thrust of her hips backward, I groaned, running the edge of my teeth over her shoulder. "I can't seem to get enough of you," I whispered against her heated skin, but the sudden rigidity of her body made me pause.

Before I could ask what was up, she said, "Do you smell that?"

With my nose buried in her hair, nuzzling the crook of her neck, all I could smell was sleep-warmed skin with a subtlety of sex musk left over from last night and Morgan's natural scent. "Mmm," I mumbled. "All I care to smell right now is you."

As I moved my thumb to flick against the quivering nub at the apex of her thighs, Morgan's hand covered mine to halt it. Snapping her legs shut tight, she leaned up on her elbow, forcing me to back away from her slightly.

"No," she whispered and turned her head so I could finally see that the usual sleepy gaze she normally wore in the morning had gone wide. "I smell smoke."

Her words broke me out of what was left of my sex-induced daze, and that's when I picked up the rankness that permeated the air. If I had paid more attention, I would have realized that the haze mixing with the daylight coming from my bedroom windows wasn't from the sun, but the smoke that was sneaking past the bottom of my bedroom door.

An explosion of broken glass set me in action.

"Oh my God!" Morgan sat up and covered her nakedness with the thin bed sheet that had only moments ago cocooned us in warmth.

Shoving my legs into a pair of worn jeans and sliding my feet into a pair of beat up running shoes, I headed for the source of the smoke. "Get dressed, stay here and be ready to move when I tell you."

"No!"

My shoulders bunched to below my ears and I spun around to face my woman. "Morgan, I need you to listen to me." The look of sheer terror on her face made me go back to her and crouch down so our eyes were even as she sat on the edge of the bed. "I don't know what I'll find on the other side of that door, but I need you to be ready for anything."

"Don't leave me," she begged.

"Never." I grabbed her face with both hands and pressed my lips firmly against hers. "I'll just be a few minutes. I need to get my phone to call the firehouse and Shane, and then I can get us the hell out of here." Getting back up to my feet, I turned to look at her from the door. "Please get dressed and be ready."

"I'm begging you, Theo, let's just get out of here. We can call 911 from my house."

She was right, but seeing as this was my turf, I had to know. With the recent happenings on Morgan's property, something niggled at the back of my mind—and that something might just have been driving an old beat up red Ford pickup truck.

Disregarding Morgan's concern and her common sense,

my hand tested the knob and when it found it cool enough—but barely—I opened the door to the hallway, letting in plumes of thick dark smoke. Grabbing a towel from the hook on the back of the door, glad that it was still moist from last night's shower I said, "Two minutes," before jumping into the hall and slamming the door shut behind me.

The first thing that hit me was the pungent smell of gasoline. With my towel over my mouth and nose, I set forward to investigate how much of the house the fire had spread to.

I didn't get far.

Without setting a foot onto the first tread of the stairwell, I could barely make out the front door due to the thick smoke and angry lashes of flames. It was too risky to even attempt heading down there. The heat was unbearable, and as I stepped back, part of the stairwell gave way with a loud crackle and snap. The hiss and sizzle of a burst water pipe was accompanied by a shooting flame heading straight for me, making me dive out of the way.

Running back toward my bedroom, I knew that my mother had been right all along. This house of mine was a fire-trap.

I sure hoped that Morgan wasn't terrified of heights.

CHAPTER 32

Trying to clear my lungs enough to take a proper deep breath, I found myself in the middle of a coughing fit as I slammed the door, secluding myself and Morgan where just moments ago we'd woken up to a total nightmare.

The woman rushed to my side, wiping at my face with the now relatively dry towel I held in my hand. The amount of soot wasn't much of a surprise.

On a wheeze I managed, "We've got to get out of here, right the fuck now."

Morgan nodded and reached for the door.

"No!" I grabbed her arm and nodded toward the window.

"You can't be serious?"

"The stairwell just gave way." I coughed some more. "The whole main floor is up in flames and if we don't hurry, I'm not even sure we'll be able to make it out of that window."

"There's no way–"

Grabbing her hands to quell her panic so she could listen to me, I said, "Baby, it's either we risk getting hurt, or we die. I'm not done living, baby, so–"

With a flicker of resolve to her impending fate, Morgan's head gave a short nod. "Okay."

Knowing the fire was reaching us at a faster rate than I would have liked, I got Morgan to crouch down on the floor to the side of the bed opposite the entrance to our safe haven while I readied myself to open the window. God only knew what would happen when the fresh air gave the fire on the other side of our wooden barrier the fuel it would need to destroy the rest of my home, my woman and me with it.

The glass panes slid up without a problem just as Morgan screamed and a wave of heat flared at my back.

"Stay down and crawl to me!" I yelled at Morgan. The bedroom door had given way to the inferno and the flames licked at the ceiling which groaned above our heads.

Despite the terror surrounding her, Morgan's body set itself in motion and she approached me. I grabbed onto her and hugged her tight before I swooped an arm under her knees and began to lift her feet-first through the opening that led to the roof above the front porch's awning. I wasn't sure it would hold, but what other choice did we have? There was no time to go out and see if the structure was still sound to bare her weight, never mind my own.

Relieved that the roof held, I tried to release Morgan but her arms held like steel rods, around my neck.

"Morg, you've got to let me go," I told her. "Crawl on your stomach to the edge and lower yourself until you can let go and fall feet-first to the ground."

"Get out and then I'll go."

"Morgan, you've got to go now!" Her head snapped back and eyes widened at my "That's an order!" Softening my tone despite my rising panic, I added, "Please, baby. I'll be right behind you."

I watched as Morgan crawled toward the edge of the roofline like a trained commando. The heat increasing in its intensity at my back, the smell of burning paint and roofing tar singeing the lining to my nose made me worry that this plan wasn't going to work.

A minute later, Morgan's worried gaze met mine as she began to lower herself over the edge of the roof. I winked, trying to reassure her that I was right behind her. "I'll see you soon."

Safety beckoned the moment my feet touched the shingles beneath me and I dropped down to lay on my front, but that sense was short lived as I reached the halfway mark to the roof's edge.

The surface I was crawling on, radiating blistering heat, gave a groan and within seconds, the shingled structure beneath my legs gave way. All I could do was dangle and hold on with my arms, or drop and hope to some higher power that I'd get out of what was quickly seeming like my peril.

CHAPTER 33

Pain.

Terror.

Heat.

Flames.

No! This isn't it!

One minute I was hanging, feeling as if I was being melted to a crisp from the inside, and the next, I became aware of a thwacking noise as my lower half swung in a rhythmic pattern.

My strength waned and my arms gave way to the agony of seized muscles and burning flesh and I dropped through the hole in the surface that should have led me to my salvation, as it had Morgan, but all I felt was the heat, my lungs begging for clean air, and whatever it was that connected with my skull as I landed.

Morgan!

As soon as her name popped into my head, her face, blackened with soot came into view armed with what looked like some old rag, which I quickly figured out was an old blanket that I'd had in the back of my truck.

She looked like a warrior. My saviour. And right then, my eyes widened with fear because she was too fucking close. What the hell was she doing?

Morgan rushed me, covered my legs with the blanket and patted to extinguish the remainder of the flames around me. When she came to grab me from under my arms, I pushed her away. "You've got to go. Leave me."

The woman ignored me, batting away my hands as she proceeded to grab hold anyway and pull.

"Morgan…"

"No! I'm not leaving you. I'm going to get you out of here and then to the hospital and then I'm going to find the motherfucker who did this and—"

At that moment, vehicles turned up the drivewayand sirens grew louder. Seconds later, Morgan yelped as she was grabbed and a second man in firefighting gear shoved his shoulder into my stomach and ran from the front step just as a loud explosion sounded.

Propane.

As I looked up, I was thankful that the crews had arrived when they had. Reduced to a pile of rubble, my home now looked better fitted to host the county's largest bonfire.

I winced the moment the guy carrying me dropped me to the ground, my head finding the softness that was Morgan's lap. "Morgan," I managed a whisper.

"Baby, it's okay." Tears streamed down her face. "We're going to be fine."

The adrenaline was fading fast and darkness beckoned. "Morg—"

"Rest," a familiar voice said, and when he pealed his mask off of his face, I became quite thankful for great friends.

"Take care of her, Ben. I don't—" The rest of my words just faded to incomprehensible mumblings until the light of day, the noises, the smells faded into nothingness.

But not before I caught a glimpse of something in the far corner of my lot, right by the tree line. A red truck. The beaten up Ford. And a man sporting nothing but a grin I would never forget.

CHAPTER 34

My throat felt hoarse, my nose dry, my body and my head ached, and my legs…

Fire! Morgan!

Trying to shoot up to a sitting position, hands pushed me back down into the mattress and my panicked state cleared enough for me to take in my surroundings, despite the coughing fit that left me gasping for air.

Along with the beeping of machines, the strong scent of antiseptic, a gasp and my own groan of pain, I realized that the nightmare was over.

"T, you're in the hospital," I heard my brother say.

I nodded. "Morgan," I said through the oxygen mask that was strapped to my face.

"She's getting patched up in the cubicle next to you," Alissa said.

Pulling the thing off of my face, I said, "I need to see her." I wasn't going to believe that she was all right until I saw her with my own eyes.

With a hiss on the other side of the curtain, I heard a female I didn't recognize say, "I want you back here tomorrow so we can change those bandages and reassess your hands, Ms. Smyth." With that, the curtain pulled away and there sat the love of my life, on the edge of a gurney, her hands wrapped up as if she was about to partake in a boxing match.

Morgan's eyes met mine and tears rushed to their surface. Before I could say anything, she rushed to my bedside and I pulled her to me. Pushing her face into my neck, I held on to her for dear life.

"I'm okay," she croaked, and tried to pull away.

"No…don't. Just a bit longer, I thought that was it for us."

Morgan's body shivered, but she spoke with a sure and steady tone. "Never."

"You were lucky, Mr. Lowell," the doctor addressed me and I looked over toward her, for the first time, noticing my parents sitting in matching chairs behind her. "Had Ms. Smyth not acted, the police said that by the time the fire trucks arrived, you could have been lost."

Nodding against Morgan's head, I kissed her cheek before letting her go and our eyes met again. *I know.* How many times had Morgan saved me since I'd met her? Once? Twice? She'd saved me from certain danger, and saved me from myself, far too many times than I can count.

Lifting her hands, so I could kiss them, I whispered the obvious. "You got hurt."

"I'd rather look like Mohammed Ali before a big fight than not have you here with me." Her voice shook with emotion.

"Mr. Lowell," the doctor interrupted us. "I'd like to talk to you about your injuries, but I have to ask that your family clear–"

Mom, Dad, my brother, and Alissa started to make their way toward the door to the room along with Morgan.

"No." I held tight to Morgan's hand. "They can stay."

With a nod, the doctor continued. "Mr. Lowell, although you've suffered a few mild burns thanks to Ms. Smyth's quick thinking, I have to caution you on that gash you suffered on the back of your head."

"What does that mean?" I asked.

"I took the liberty of reading your military file, Theo," she said. "Burns and severe smoke inhalation aside, the concussion you suffered might be moderate, but more than enough to have caused you permanent damage, or killed you, with your history."

I nodded my understanding. None of it was news to me.

"With that said, I'd like to keep you in here for the next day so we can monitor your progress. As for the rest of your injuries, there's a rather sizeable burn where part of your jeans melted to your thigh which will leave a scar, but—"

"Doc, do I look like I'm worried about scarring?" I gave her an incredulous look. "With all due respect, I'm not new to them, if you paid enough attention to my medical records." *Just as long as I can still walk to get down the aisle when—*

I was cut off by a gasp coming from none other than Morgan herself, which was my first indication that I'd spoken my last thought aloud. Mom was bubbling over with excitement as she clutched onto Morgan's shoulders, hugging the woman to her while Dad, Theo, and Alissa were all grinning like the cat that ate the cream.

My head throbbed, causing me to wince, when I forgot myself and shook it at everyone's antics.

The pretty doctor lady blushed, but smiled warmly. "That shouldn't be a problem, but I do have to caution you on proper care—"

"Do you mind if we pick up on that a little later, like when you're ready to discharge me?" I asked, my eyes stuck on Morgan. "My woman seems a little surprised at my runaway mouth and before she runs out of here where I can't follow her, I'd like to reassure her that it's me and not the painkillers talking."

Chuckling, she nodded. "Sure."

"Come here, baby." I motioned for Morgan to sit beside me on my hospital bed. Mom had to give her a little push to set her in motion, but she came freely. "Guys, I appreciate your being here, but I think I need a little time alone with Morgan."

"Sure, brother," Paxton said and quickly escorted Alissa out of the room.

"We'll be back later with dinner," Mom said, and Dad added, "You couldn't have picked a better one, son."

"I know, Dad." I grinned at the blush that flared over Morgan's features and waited to hear the soft click of our hospital room door shut. Flushed and stunned to silence, that was the sight of the woman who held my forever in her hands. I definitely couldn't have chosen better.

I had all but two minutes with Morgan, and not much of a chance to explain myself, when Shane walked into the room.

Luckily, it looked like Morgan hadn't been spooked by my earlier slip of the tongue, and now sat cuddled against me in the bed.

"T," he said, relief in his eyes, which was quickly chased away by a wide grin. "I have to say you sure as hell know how to keep me busy. Glad you're both okay."

I grabbed on to his outstretched hand and gave it a squeeze. "Can't say I'm happy about that, bro. Find anything out?"

"The fire's out, but I can't say there's much left but ashes and assorted distorted metal and pieces of wood," he said. "Any idea what could have happened?"

I went with my gut and told him. "That was no accident."

The man's nod was one of understanding. "What makes you say that?"

"I smelled gasoline when I first left the bedroom to investigate." Somehow I knew there was something more, but my head was throbbing and my memory was foggy.

"Why didn't you just leave right away?"

"I was half asleep," I defended. "I didn't notice until after Morgan pointed out the smell."

"Ms. Smyth–"

"Morgan, please."

Shane smiled. "Morgan…why didn't you wake Theo up?"

Morgan's mouth dropped and I was quick to jump in to

answer my friend's question. "I was awake before her, so if you're looking at any of us to point the finger at for failing to notice anything, then you lay the blame on me, Shane. I–"

"I'm not blaming anyone, I'm just trying to make sense out of all of this, T." He ran his hand through his hair, leaving it sticking out at all angles. "One of my men saw an old beat up Ford truck that matched your description, not too far up the road from Morgan's property."

"Did you find the guy?" I asked, the picture of that grinning face becoming clearer as the seconds trickled by.

He shook his head. "By the time word got to me, it was gone, but we've got plate numbers that match the partials that Morgan spotted the night her house was vandalized."

"I saw him."

"What?" Morgan sat up abruptly.

"Right before I blacked out. Something about him is familiar, but I'm not sure." I rubbed my temples to soothe the ache, hoping it would help me think. "There was something in his smile, something about the look he had. I've seen it before. He's behind all of what's going on."

Shane was writing all of this down. "I've got CSU working on it, T. With the way this guy's escalating, I'd say we'll be on top of him soon. His behavior is erratic. Since I'm technically here as a friend and not in an official capacity right now, let's change the subject, shall we?" The man's gaze went from me to Morgan and his lips went from a straight line to a full-blown grin. "So, Morgan, how'd a lady like you end up with some rough guy like him?"

"Don't play into it, baby," I said, but the woman ignored me.

"It's easy, Shane." She looked at me, a twinkle of humor appearing in her eyes and turned back to the man.

"Go on." He leaned forward.

"All I had to do was ask him…"

She paused for dramatic effect, but Shane was too impatient. "Ask him what?" He lifted his cup of coffee up to his mouth, his eyes never leaving hers.

"Well, to plug up my hole of course," she said as he was mid-sip.

The man coughed and sputtered, his coffee dribbling down his chin and shirt. Morgan giggled and I found myself joining in the laughter as the man grabbed a few tissues from the bedside table and tried to mop up his mess.

By the time the laughter faded, I was feeling the weight of slumber begin to take me, and I cursed the painkillers in my system.

Shane noticed this and patted my shoulder. "You rest up, T. I'll drop by later." As he got up, he leaned over and kissed the top of Morgan's head. "I think you'll do this guy a hell of a lot of good, Morgan Smyth. Feel better, and take care of him."

By then, I couldn't keep my eyes open, but I heard Morgan's "I plan to," before my senses left me again.

A while later, I woke up to hushed chatter at my bedside. Imagine my surprise when I found Dalton and Brycen keeping Morgan entertained.

"Oh look, sleeping beauty is awake!" Brycen smirked.

"I see Shane's activated the telephone chain." I looked toward Morgan to find her looking tired, but happy. "How are you feeling, sweetheart? Have these two been telling tales?"

Dalton harrumphed as Morgan explained. "No, they're here because Shane thinks they can be of help."

My brows reached for my hairline as I turned toward Dalton. "How?"

It turns out that after Dalton was medically discharged from the Rangers, he'd decided to take the inheritance money left to him by his grandfather and open his own security firm. Apparently Shane liked to use him from time to time when resources were stretched too thin, or when he needed answers that came easier by slightly unorthodox means.

"Most of the guys work fulltime, but I have a few, like

Cade, who will handle a few cases for me when I need them."

Brycen jumped in. "Don't worry, T, we'll figure out who this guy is and—"

"We?" I looked between Dalton and Brycen. "You work for him too?"

"I'd be crazy to let him go anywhere else." Dalton chuckled. "His talents were wasted with the FBI."

My eyes widened. "Are you kidding me right now?"

Brycen slapped Dalton on the back. "Nope. When Dalton came back and told me what his plans were, I jumped on board. He needed someone of my talents, and let's face it, I make better money with our contracts than I did working for the government."

"You'll have to stop on by the office and check things out when everything settles down." Dalton grinned. "I've got some toys I know you're going to want to see."

Knowing him and his love for weapons, I knew the man would never disappoint.

Half an hour later, after a whole lot of reminiscing that had Morgan bowled over in stitches, Dalton and Brycen took their leave to meet up with Shane who was going to share the details of what Morgan and I have been going through. I may have faith in our justice system, but I have to say that I felt better knowing that my guys had my back.

CHAPTER 35

It took another day before the doctor allowed me to go home. Add to that a second day Morgan and I waited for results from Shane and his CSU team, not to mention the arson department, as well as Dalton.

That's two days where no answers came.

Two days surrounded by family and friends, and Morgan waiting on me hand and foot, which only made me laugh because with every effort, I ended up having to help her out since her hands were still bandaged and of not much use.

Due to all of the above, and doctor's orders, that was also two days without being able to show Morgan any physical attention, which was wearing thin on me.

"I wish we could have gone somewhere else," I mumbled from the driver's seat as Morgan's van putted down my brother's driveway, coming to a stop close to the front steps. I'd have preferred my truck, but as much as it had escaped the fire, it hadn't the explosion. Suffice to say, my ride was stuck in the body repair shop for the next couple of weeks.

"I know," Morgan said as I got out and ran around to the passenger side to help her out. "I would have liked to have gone home too, but Pax is right. If something were to happen, with the state we're in–"

"Hey," I wrapped my arms around her waist, pulling her against me so our fronts made contact as I leaned back into the side of the car, "I'm not some weak old man, sweetheart."

Her hand came up to cup my cheek and I rubbed my two days' worth of scruff over her gauze-covered skin. "I know, but I feel better knowing that we have backup here, just in case. And what if something happened to you? I couldn't handle–"

My lips collided with hers, ceasing Morgan's words. Truth was, as annoyed as I was for being surrounded around the clock by family, I was relieved, knowing that we were safer in numbers. As much as I'd like to claim myself invincible, something about this concussion had me worried. It seemed like it was taking an eternity for the throbbing in my head and dizziness spells to dissipate. And let's not forget the memory issues. Things from the day of the fire were still a bit hazy. I knew that the man I'd seen hadn't been a figment of my imagination. I knew him from somewhere, it's the only way he could have seemed familiar. Maybe from now until the time I was back on my feet, my head would clear up enough and we'd be able to get some answers, put a stop to this chaos long enough for Morgan and I to enjoy our relationship and plan for the future—one that was about figuring out vows, living arrangements, a family—and not one about wondering if we would still be in danger of losing one another tomorrow or not.

The door opened for us as we reached it, an excited Jasper jumping on the balls of his feet awaited us. "Is it true, Uncle Theo?" I could have used some of the kid's energy right then. "Are you and Morgan having a sleepover?"

Morgan ruffled Jasper's hair. "That's right, sweetie. Uncle Theo and me are going to be sleeping over for a little while. Is that okay?"

"Awesome!" The boy moved to the side and let us enter the house. "We can play in the back yard, build a fort, wrestle, and–"

"Jasper." Alissa came to meet us, shaking her head at her stepson. "Leave Morgan and your uncle alone. There'll be time to play later."

The boy could have won an award for 'world's best-behaved child,' had one existed, what with the complete turnaround he did. I promised myself that the kid would get a reward for his efforts before my stay was up.

"Are you sure you two will be fine for the next two hours?" Paxton asked.

"Go ahead," I heard Morgan tell him. "Having a quiet house for the next few hours will help Theo rest up better."

"We're only five minutes out, ten if we're out for a ride with Dad," my brother said.

"Go have fun, and tell your folks we say hi," Morgan said.

I heard what must have been the front door closing and hoped that Morgan had the good sense to lock it behind them.

Silence filled the air until I heard footsteps heading straight for me. Morgan's floral scent hit me first, and then I felt the dip in the mattress before her front plastered itself gently against my left side.

"Hey," I whispered to let her know I was awake.

Her chocolate orbs held a hint of apology. "Did I wake you?"

"Thank you for assuring them that going for a few hours would be fine." I kissed her forehead. "I'm glad we have some time alone."

"It's been pretty scarce, huh?"

I grunted. "That's an understatement."

A padded hand ran circles over my abdomen. "How are you feeling?"

"Happy," was the first thing out of my mouth.

She giggled. "That's not what I meant."

Maybe it was time I showed her what my answer was, instead of telling her.

Pushing my knee between her legs, I slowly put pressure on Morgan's shoulder so she rolled to her back, in turn granting me with the capability to cover her body with mine.

"I feel like I'm on top of something wonderful," I whispered against her ear, feeling her body quiver as my teeth clamped lightly on its lobe. "I feel like I can do anything when I'm around you." I trailed my lips to just below her jaw. "I feel grateful that we're alive." With a nuzzle to her collarbone, I wrapped my left hand around her thigh, hiking up her leg and hugging it around the side of my hip before letting my fingers slip inside the bottom hem of her t-shirt. Looking down at Morgan, I finally said, "Baby, I feel like if I don't make love to you, right here, right now—"

"Please," was all I needed to hear before I slammed my mouth to hers in a fierce kiss that held all the pent-up passion, lust, and frustration that couldn't be released over the last few days.

Morgan's hands reached for the hem of my shirt in an attempt to pull it off of me. I laughed at her helpless expression, reminding me of a kitten batting at a toy with its paws.

"A little help here," she grumbled and I helped her with both our shirts, her shorts following immediately and then, with a little difficulty, I managed to lower mine.

Taking my cock in hand, I guided my length to her heat. "You're soaked," I groaned against her cheek and felt her legs tighten against my ass, pulling me inside her after I'd breached her entrance.

The slow forward glide that let me feel the whole of her silken sheath had me grinding my teeth, my eyes clamping shut in an effort not to burst prematurely.

"I love you," Morgan whispered. "Open your eyes, Theo."

At her gentle command, I obeyed and realized something…I'd found everything I could have ever wanted in life. "Oh fuck but I love you too," came whooshing out as all of me was finally cocooned within her. Was there any other feeling that bested the one of being this close to Morgan? No, I was pretty sure there wasn't.

CHAPTER 36

"Marry me," I whispered against the skin of Morgan's neck.

Yes, without a ring, without romance, without a special dinner reservation or place of significance that either of us held dear in our hearts. It was simply Morgan, cradled in my arms after a long sought-after bout of mind-numbing sex, covered in the thin sheet, the sun setting through the window, being the sole source of lighting in the room in that moment.

Morgan's head shot up. "What did you say?"

As she perched herself over my chest on her elbows, my hand pushed a loose strand of hair and tucked it behind her ear as I studied her expression. "Marry me, Morgan Smyth," I repeated. "I know it's fast, but we've been through so much. I can live without you, but I refuse to, because I don't want a future without you in it, baby."

"Theo…" Her voice trailed.

"I know I'm screwing this up. But I don't want to wait until I'm well enough to have Paxton come with me to pick out the perfect ring, then set up some elaborate scheme to woo you and then knock your socks off with some over-the-top surprise, that will have me worried would fail to be perfect, just to speak what's in my heart."

The tear that escaped her put a halt to my words.

"You would do that?"

I shook my head with incredulity. "Of course I would. In a heartbeat." I sighed. Didn't she have any idea what I was willing to do, to go through, just to have her with me? "You deserve everything I can give you, and most definitely more. And if you let me, I'll spend the rest of my days making sure you're as happy as you could ever imagine being."

"Yes."

"Huh?" Her answer hadn't yet sunk in because I had been trying to piece together more words to prove the lengths to which I was willing to go to ensure she would agree to be mine until death parted us.

Her teary giggle had me grinning. "Yes, Theo, I'll marry you."

My eyes widened at the significance of it all. "You will?"

"You bet your fine chiselled ass I will, baby." She lowered her face until her lips brushed mine on her next words. "I don't care what you think I deserve, all I need is you, Theodore Lowell."

With a hand wrapped around the back of her neck, I tilted my head up just enough to lightly peck her lips. "Then soon, we'll go out and find you a ring, because right now, I'm showing my unofficial bride-to-be how thankful I am that she's chosen me over every other shmuck out there."

An hour later, we were cuddled together on the couch watching a movie when my brother walked in, followed by the clamour of his family.

He lifted a large Tupperware container. "Mom gave me this for you and Morgan. She made chicken fried steak, dumplings and her special gravy."

As if right on cue, my stomach grumbled.

Morgan smirked. "I think we can use a little sustenance, don't you?"

"M-hmm."

Paxton met his wife's gaze and then grinning, looked at us. "So what did you two get up to while we were out?" He handed me the food container while Alissa held the baby and sent Jasper to the kitchen to fetch forks.

"Lots of laying down," I said, but the grin I failed to hide from my face said it all, and my brother humorously shook his head, sporting a grin of his own.

"Uh-huh," Alissa muttered, "I bet. Were you even cleared for that kind of laying?"

Morgan buried her face into my neck with an embarrassed groan while I grinned, and my brother guffawed before adding, "Like that would stop him. Sure as hell wouldn't stop me."

With the baby quieted down for the night, the rest of us settled in for some lighthearted conversation.

Jasper turned from his movie and gave me the stink-eye. "Morgan's not a baby, she can feed herself you know."

Morgan giggled with her mouthful of chicken and held up her bandaged hands while she chewed her food and swallowed. "Your uncle knows that, and I'm sure I could have done just fine but–"

"I like taking care of her, buddy," I finished for her. "I can't be up and about like I normally am so we trade off. I feed her and she can go get stuff for me."

The child seemed to ponder that for a minute.

Paxton harrumphed. "You're just being lazy."

"I think it's sweet." Alissa cuddled into my brother's side. Paxton looked down at his wife, eyebrow arched. "What? Are you telling me that you wouldn't be doing the same thing if the situation was reversed and it were us?"

Morgan snorted. "She's got you there, Pax. You know you'd be twice as bad if that were the case. Allie's told me about how you were with her after her marrow donation. And what about the time she went into false labor with Abigail and you–"

Paxton grumbled, but gave it a little thought. "Okay, okay…you're right," he said and kissed his wife's forehead. "I'd do it all for you, you wouldn't have to lift a finger." He kissed her cheek. "Or a toe." He kissed her other cheek.

Jasper put a stop to the commotion with over-exaggerated

gagging sounds and then with a whiny stretched out, "Dad," and everyone found themselves laughing.

As Morgan, Alissa, and Paxton settled into a conversation of their own while Jasper watched the end of a movie, I remained silent, enjoying the mood of the day.

I hadn't realized what I was doing until Morgan snuggled in closer to me, bending her head up to peck my cheek.

Smiling down at her, her eyes shone with so much happiness that I could feel it warm me from the inside. "Soon," I whispered as I continued to swipe my thumb back and forth where my ring would be sitting.

She nodded, kissed my mouth lightly and repeated, "Soon," at a whisper.

CHAPTER 37

Three days after our release from hospital, Shane was knocking on my brother's door.

"Anything?" I asked the man as I led him to the living room. Morgan automatically set down her e-reader and got up to shake his hand before offering him something to drink.

"The report on the fire investigation was on my desk this morning. It's arson. Hell, you two are lucky to have made it out from what I read. The Chief said he had no idea how that fire didn't light up the entire sky within minutes."

The hair on the back of my neck prickled. Grabbing onto Morgan's hand, she automatically leaned into my side, a shiver racking her entire body.

"We've been keeping an eye out on your place too, Morgan," he announced.

"Why?"

"I asked him to, baby," I said. "Everything happens wherever I'm at."

"Except for the night you went out," she pointed out.

"True."

"We found fresh tracks on both your properties. Something that could belong to a Ford truck, I suppose. I've got my men on it." Shane leaned forward on his knees before reaching into his jacket and pulling out a Ziploc bag with the word *evidence* on its seal. "This is the part you're really not going to like." He set it down on the coffee table, sliding it over to Morgan and I.

As if the wording wasn't enough, the writing of the short

note couldn't have been described as anything but furious: *This isn't over.*

On a hissing gasp, I realized that my grip on Morgan's hand had tightened to the point of pain and I let go, bellowing a, "Sonofabitch!"

Morgan shot to her feet and left the room, heading toward the kitchen.

"I think I've made a mistake here, T," Shane said. "Whoever this guy is, he knows both of you. This is personal."

"Well, the only person that ever did is dead, Shane," I said.

"Um..."

Shane and I turned to find Morgan standing there, wringing the hell out of her hands.

"Morgan?" Shane said at the same time I said, "Baby, if you're thinking that–"

"Hell no, Theo!" She shook her head, a look of disbelief settling on her face. "I *know* it's not my brother. You've told me the entire story...I've seen his body...I know it's not him, but..."

"Morgan, if you know something, even if you think it's a stretch, you need to tell us." Shane gave her his best 'no-bullshit' look.

The woman began to pace, her fingers running into her hair, pulling at it as she mumbled to herself. "It can't be." She paused to look at me. "He would have been back by now, if–" She resumed her pacing only to stop and look at me, her brow furrowed. "How did you say Rick died?"

I took the two steps that led me to stand in front of Morgan, my hands reaching for her shoulders. "I'm not liking where this is going, Morgan. I don't know how he died, but he was captured with me. Why?"

"Shane, sit down." The man did as Morgan ordered, his eyes meeting mine with a questioning look. "Theo, I need you to think about it for a second." She broke my hold and pushed me so I sat on the couch.

"Morgan, I can't talk about that mission more than what I've already told you."

"Well, let me just tell you what I'm thinking, and then you can make that judgement call, will you!" she snapped. I nodded and let her continue. "Theo, they never had a body to ship back for him, did they?"

I shook my head. "How'd you know?"

"I can't believe I never clued in to this until now." She sounded disgusted with herself.

"What?" This came from Shane.

"Donnelly, Theo," she whispered, her eyes widening as did mine. "Baby, your Rick is *my* Richard!"

Shane looked lost, but that's when everything clicked for me. That was the link that tied us together. The fact that one of my former men was one and the same as Morgan's good-for-nothing and abusive ex-fiancé had my blood boiling.

"We never really discussed Rick…Richard in full length past what he did to me. You mentioned his last name a few times but it never clicked until now. Being Richard's next of kin, I only got his dog tags," Morgan explained. "Theo, you weren't there after the capture. Can you really claim it's that far-fetched of an idea? Fuck, everyone thought you were dead for three years! All there ever was of you were your tags, too."

She had a point. A too-fucking-valid one at that.

"So, what are we dealing with here?" Shane asked.

Morgan looked at me as I answered for us both. "A ghost."

CHAPTER 38

"Are you sure you're doing what's best?" Paxton asked as he helped me load up the back of his truck. When I loaded the cooler with the rest of the provisions we would need for the next week, I lifted the tailgate and turned to my brother.

"We can't stay here, P. As if it's not enough that we're putting you and Alissa out, the longer we stay, I'm worried that something could happen to your family," I explained to him. "I wouldn't be able to live with myself if something happened to any of you."

"Do you think this'll work?"

I looked past my brother, seeing Alissa and Morgan hugging. *I hope so.* "Dalton thinks it will. I trust him. Promise me something, P." He nodded as I reached for him and crushed him in a hug. "If anything happens to me, make sure that Morgan gets out of this and lives a life I would have been honored to have lived with her."

"Don't talk like that." Paxton was choked up. Hell, so was I. "You'll get through this. You're the toughest sonofabitch I know. Dude, you're like a fucking cat." His chuckle lacked any humor, but it did lighten the mood a little.

"I'm not sure I'm supposed to have nine lives, brother, but I swear to you that I'm not staying gone for good. It's just in case."

"I get it, T. We'll be here if you need us." Paxton backed up, slapped my shoulder, then reached into his pocket. "By the way…here." He chucked the tiny parcel at me.

I shoved the item in my pocket and patted it. "Thanks for looking after that."

Morgan came to my side and I slid my arm around her shoulders.

"Ready?" she asked.

"Loaded. Just waiting on you." I kissed her temple.

After she hugged Paxton, thanking him for their hospitality, I held the passenger side door open for her to get in, then closed it. My feet were on the running board when Paxton shouted, "Don't wait!"

You're right, P. Life's too short.

"Do you think this'll work?" Morgan asked after we brought in the last of our belongings.

"If it doesn't, I don't know what will." I dropped the box of canned goods on the rickety kitchenette table as Morgan shut the cabin's door. Turning to her, she walked right into my arms.

"So, what do you suppose we do as we wait for him to make his move?" Her palms skimmed upward on my chest.

Palming her jean-clad cheeks, I hitched her up in my arms, Morgan's legs wrapping around my hips. "I can think of a few things."

"Smoke signals?" She smirked.

"With the way you set me on fire, woman, we'd burn this place down."

Two days later, three quarters of an hour away from Jacksonville, in a cabin deep in the woods, Morgan made us a dinner of sandwiches, while I started a fire in the hearth to ward off the chill of the evening.

The waiting game, the not knowing what would happen next, weighed heavily on me, but I can also say that the undisrupted one-on-one time with Morgan had been my own version of heaven.

"Any word from Shane?" Morgan handed me my

plate before settling next to me on the floor, against the couch.

I nodded. "Brycen managed to find the owner of the truck based on the partial plates. Shane said he sent a cruiser to the address. They found the owner dead of a shotgun wound, execution style." Morgan gasped and set her plate to the side, her appetite clearly lost. "We don't know what the link between them is yet." I dug my cell out of my pocket to make sure that the signal was still strong, impatient for more news. As I was about to set it aside, it rang. My brows furrowed. "It's Pax." Looking down at the device, I slid my finger against the screen to answer. "P?"

"He took Jasper! Motherfucker took my son, T!"

"Fuck! We're on our way. Sit tight, brother, and dammit, don't do anything stupid, and if you haven't, call Shane." Disconnecting the call, my phone dropped to the carpet as a pain-filled cry escaped me. The bastard had gone too far.

CHAPTER 39

Cars, trucks, SUVs and two police cruisers were all parked half-hazardly in my brother's driveway by the time Morgan and I got there.

Rushing the front steps, an officer I didn't recognize halted me before I had the chance to get through the door. Instead of having to deal with assault on an officer by clocking him out of sheer frustration, I hollered for my brother.

In his stead, Shane came out. "Theo—"

"Let me in there, man."

"I need you to calm down."

"Don't tell me to calm down, that bastard's gone too far! It's time to end this right-the-fuck-now!"

Kayla came rushing out the front door, toward Morgan. "I'm so sorry," she kept repeating. Her being there didn't make sense. Nothing did.

"Kayla?" The woman turned to face me. The fear in her eyes made me ask, "Am I missing something? Why are you here? What aren't you all telling me?"

Paxton, myself, Dalton, Cade, Brycen, an assortment of my brother's friends, Shane, and a few of his law enforcement buddies were all gathered around the kitchen table, trying to figure out a plan of action.

"He's going to call," Shane stated to the room, then met my eye. "Jasper's just the bargaining chip to get to you and Morgan, Theo." There was a shared grunt of agreement, one which I didn't join, as I was too busy feeling guilty for what my return had caused for my brother. Then again, I can't imagine how little Savannah was dealing with her guilt when Jasper had been snatched right in front of her.

I knew that they were of the same age, that they attended the same school, even, but I had no idea that the two were close friends. Savannah had explained how *Uncle Richie* had approached them after school. He'd wanted to play a game of hide and seek. It was plausible to a six-year-old, when you think about it. The kids didn't hesitate one bit, ignoring all those stranger danger lessons that their elders had taught them, since one of them knew the person.

"He said that the boys would hide and that I'd have to look for them." The little girl's bottom lip quivered as she recounted the events, sitting on her mother's lap. "But them Mom came to pick me up, and when I called out to them to come out, because Mom was there, they didn't. Now I'm in trouble."

Crouching down so we were face-to-face, I grabbed her hand. "Shorty, you're not in trouble," I tried to reassure her. "If it weren't for you, we wouldn't know what happened."

The little one sniffled, then threw herself into my arms. Kayla's tearful eyes met mine.

"You'll find him, right, Theo? You'll find Jasper and bring him back?" the little girl begged.

"You know I will," I swore. "I promise."

Handing Savannah back to her mother, I noticed that we were one person short. "Where's Morgan?"

Nicole came into the kitchen, heading for the fridge. She'd been with the women in the living room. "She got a call, took it outside because of the noise."

My blood ran cold. "What? When?"

"Ten minutes or so ago?" she answered.

"Fuck!" I made a run for the front door only to see a red Ford truck, fishtailing at the end of the driveway before it turned away from town.

Running for Paxton's truck, since I still had his keys, I jump in around the same time Dalton opened the passenger door and did the same, slamming it behind him. Shock at his presence had me staring at him.

"Go!" he hollered, whipping out what must have been his service weapon, and begins loading it. "If you think that you're going at it alone, think again. I've got your back, brother."

"Thanks, Kippers."

Seconds onto the road, my cell rings and I throw it to Kippers to answer. The man puts it on speaker.

"T?" It's Paxton.

"Yeah."

"Shotgun's in behind the backseat. Shells are locked in the glove compartment."

"Got it!"

"Shane's on your tail with Cade, and Brycen is on his heels."

"Okay."

"Don't do anything stupid, T."

"I can't guarantee that, brother. Love you."

"Be safe. Love you too."

As soon as Paxton disconnects, my foot floors the gas. The cavalry was behind me in the form of a former army ranger, a police detective, a search and rescue worker, and a programming specialist.

CHAPTER 40

I was coming up on what were the charred remains of my home when I chose to call it quits. There was no dust trail. We hadn't met up with any other vehicles on the way. I was losing hope, and fast, and the fading daylight wasn't helping as nighttime was setting in.

Pulling over into my driveway, the only thing left to greet me was the old dilapidated barn, even worse for wear, most likely from the blast of the propane tank when it exploded.

I stopped the truck and got out, the rest of the guys catching up with me within a few minutes. Shane was the first to approach me.

"You can't just go off half-cocked, Theo!"

I got in the man's face. "What would you have done? You're not the one who saw him drive off with the only person that's made you feel like you were worth a damn, Shane!"

"Guys!" Dalton limped, weapon drawn, toward the barn. His gaited walk grew to a full out sprint within seconds. "We've got something!" The man pried the door open, revealing the one vehicle we'd thought we'd lost, it's chrome bumper shining due to the headlights aimed at it.

"We've got a visual on the Ford," Shane said into his lapel radio, coming to a stop beside Dalton. "Cancel the APB on…" I tuned him out as I knew he'd rattle off the license plate number, make, and every other detail to the vehicle.

"Hold up!" This was Cade, who looked as if he was sniffing the air around him, then mumbled something to Dalton who bent over to peer under the truck with the Maglite on his keychain.

I moved closer, circling the vehicle, but giving it a wide berth because I could now smell what Cade had, and I know I wasn't storing any of that shit in here. Gasoline.

"Shane?" The man in question was still on his radio, his brows furrowed as he looked up. "If I didn't know what to look for, I wouldn't have noticed it, but let them know this truck is rigged to blow," Dalton said, he and Cade slowly exiting the barn, but not before Dalton's beam flashed on something in the far corner, by the dried up piles of wooden boards, and few bales of hay that hadn't been arranged that way the last time I'd been in here.

"Give me that!" I ripped Dalton's Maglite out of his hands, aiming it into the corner to get a better look as Cade said, "We've got fresh tracks leading past the side of the barn. He's got another ride, and my guess is he took the access road behind your property to get away." That explained why we hadn't seen anything for the last five miles or so.

"Has anyone thought to check Morgan's garage? Her brother's car is stored in there," I said as I moved toward the corner I'm observing.

"Listen." Shane turns to me as I continued my approach. "I just got word that some anonymous source has picked up chatter online. It seems that our guy's been boasting."

Brycen said, "Anything I can do to help?" as I held my index finger up to my lips, then pointed to the corner.

As I crouched down, I heard a whimper.

"Fuck! There's someone under this shit," I announced and motioned for Dalton to give me a hand. "I need for the rest of you to get back. Who knows if he's as sick as to rig this pile to go up too."

Cade, Shane and Brycen stayed where they were, regardless of my warnings.

"Theo, he's posted photos of what he's done. We know it's him for sure." Shane seemed to be assessing how I was dealing with his latest information before telling me more, but at this point, I was only half-hearing him. I needed to maintain my focus on the task at hand. For all I knew, there was a pressure censor beneath all this rubble and whoever was under–

"Jasper!" It came out as a whisper when my nephew's face was revealed.

"Dispatch, this is Detective Peters."

"Go ahead, Detective."

"I need an ambulance at…" I tuned him out as I took in the little boy before me. Jasper was a teary mess, pale, gagged, and shaking. Judging by his lack of movement, he was either bound or injured. The thought of the latter being the case chilled my blood.

"Hold on, Jasper," I choked out. "We'll get you out of there as quick as we can, okay?" The nod was there, but only slight. I reached for the folding knife I always kept in my pocket. "I'm going to cut this gag first so we can talk. Don't move an inch, buddy."

"The bad man's got Morgan!" came out of Jasper's mouth as soon as the gag left it.

"I know, buddy, I know." I turned to Dalton who'd been inspecting the pile of wooden rubble as I was handling Jasper. "How's it look?"

The man was relieved, but I could tell that he was worried that he'd missed something. Pressure sure as hell was on when the victim was someone you knew. "I don't see anything."

"I want out, Uncle Theo."

"We're working on it." And a thought occurred to me. "Jasp, can you tell me if the bad man put anything in there with you? Were you awake when he did this?"

"He just told me that we'd play another game of hide-and-seek. He said that if I wasn't found, then it would all be your fault if I died." The boy's tears, which had calmed, started up again. "He didn't say that last part really loud, but I heard him."

"Shh…" I reassured him. Or tried to. "Is there anything under there with you?"

His whimpered, "No," had my breath cutting short.

With a nod, Dalton and I began to remove each board, one at a time. "Buddy, you let me know if something is hurting and we'll stop, okay?"

"I'm okay." He bit his lower lip. "I knew you'd find me. You really are a hero!" Dalton snorted, which had Jasper turning his gaze to him. "Are you one of them too? You look like you could be one of them. What happened to your leg? Are you hurt?"

"Jasper–" I started to say but the static from Shane's lapel radio interrupted me.

"Detective Peters, this is Connie at dispatch."

"You got an ETA on that ambo, Connie?"

"They're ten minutes out. We just got another call from our anonymous source. More photos were posted within the last fifteen minutes. He's got eyes on you, Detective."

"I want those photos, Connie."

"Ten-four. I've sent them to your cruiser's computer. You should have them in a few minutes along with the site's link."

"Thanks. I want to know the minute this person reaches out again. I want to talk to them directly, you hear? Over and out." Shane rushed to his car, sat sideways in his driver's seat and unlocked his computer as Dalton released Jasper from the last of the boards. The little boy jumped into my arms and tightened his arms around my neck like a vice, sobs finally surfacing.

"Sonofabitch!" Cade was the first to say as I followed the men's lead.

"This was within the last half hour!" Dalton stated.

The sick fuck was playing a game that had my head spinning, my temper flaring, and my body aching to pound something. "How the fuck is he here and we can't see–"

"He's not," Brycen leaned over Shane's shoulder and pointed at the shot of all of us surrounding and facing the barn. "The angle's all wrong. Unless this guy is up a tree, he's not here."

"And he would have been made by now. This place is wide open until you get to the surrounding woods, there's no way he could have left here after we'd arrived," I thought aloud, then turned to Brycen and asked, "No one look, but I'll just go on record by saying remote activated cameras?"

He nodded. "Nighttime vision ones."

I groaned. "You think you can trace its signal on one of those supercomputers of yours?"

The man grinned. "You know I can. You're lucky I never leave home without one."

CHAPTER 41

Paxton's home had once again been designated as our command post. The police cruisers were gone and only Shane, Dalton, Cade, Brycen and myself remained. Kayla, Savannah, Mom, and Dad had all gone to meet with Paxton and Alissa at the hospital to be with Jasper.

The boy had a few minor scratches and bruises, but I feared for the psychological repercussions. PTSD could wreak havoc on an adult, and I didn't even want to fathom what it could do to a child. Suffice to say, when everything blew over, when Morgan was in my arms again, and Rick where he should have been all of this time, which is six feet under, I'd be keeping a close watch on my nephew. This was my fault. I'd shoulder the blame, but I'd put things right again, or die trying.

Congregated around Paxton's dining room table, Brycen blurts out, "I think I might be on to something."

Shane spoke my thoughts aloud. "I hope so."

At this point, I was well on my way to wearing out the room's hardwood flooring with my pacing. Forty-five minutes earlier, when he'd evidently seen we'd gotten to Jasper, Rick began broadcasting a live feed of Morgan.

I damn well nearly lost my mind at what I saw.

Bound, gagged, and if the camera was recording anything other than a black and white coloring, I'd say she was pale. Her makeup had run down her face, her eyes were puffy from tears, undoubtedly, but despite this, it was the split in her lip, not to mention the gash on her cheek that sent my emotions into a tailspin. I wanted blood. What was worse, I wanted to end every single motherfucker out there who was viewing this shit. The sentiment only grew as the number of views climbed at a rapid rate.

"Gotcha!" Brycen turns toward all of us after an hour of tapping away furiously at his laptop.

"Tell me you've got a location." I wasn't above begging at this point.

"Not quite, but I've managed to trace the camera's IP address. Bastard didn't even have the fucking thing encrypted," Brycen explained. Then his laptop chimed. "What the–" The man chuckled. Here I am, in the fight of my life, no knowledge of how to find my woman, and he's busy laughing!

"So help me God, Bryce, but–" I started to say.

"Guys, I got our Little Helper on task, or so it seems."

After a minute of tapping away at his keyboard, Brycen looked at me. "It's Morgan. She's got a lead on Morgan."

It took another twenty minutes of Brycen working with his new cohort to triangulate the camera's signal.

I ran my hands through my hair, pulling at the tresses. "What's taking so long?" I knew what it was since Brycen mentioned that despite the no encryption thingy, the camera's signals were being pinged off of dummy towers, or something like that. Sue me for not knowing the damn lingo, but I trusted the man to find my woman.

My phone rang.

"Morgan?" I put the phone on speaker.

"Find me yet?"

"Listen, you sick sonofabitch–"

"Tsk, tsk, tsk..." Rick's voice lost all humor. "No, *you* listen! If you want her back, you're going to do as I ask, Lowell." The coppery flavor of blood came as I bit down on my lip too hard, waiting for him to continue. "If you didn't want me to know you found me, you should have told your boy to beef up his system. Tell everyone to back off, Lowell, or you'll be losing another team. I'll call in an hour with a meetup." The line went dead.

Brycen motioned for me to look at his screen. I began to read.

> **YTh@tHussy:** Stop what ur doing
> **V@p0r:** ?
> **YTh@tHussy:** Seconds away from…
> **V@p0r:** ?
> **V@p0r:** Away from what?
> **YTh@tHussy:** GOT IT!

"Fuck!" Brycen slammed a fist on the tabletop. At this point, everyone was hovering over the man's shoulders. Brycen's feed to the video had gone dark. The only thing that seemed to be working was his chat screen.

> **V@p0r:** Everything's gone black.

Brycen gripped his hair and groaned. "I can't believe I got made." Everyone waited for a response and got nothing, so Brycen began to type into the chat screen.

> **V@p0r:** Talk 2 me Huss
> **YTh@tHussy:** lol had to shut you down

"*She* shut you down?" Dalton seemed surprised at this. "Fuck, man, did you have to pick today for your skills to be lacking?"

I couldn't have agreed more with my friend's statement.

> **YTh@tHussy:** Hold on. 1 sec.
> **V@por:** Don't have that. Why'd you do that?

YTh@tHussy: Richlands hwy, lot 5

Shane rattled off the address over his radio, demanding that cars be sent to check things out, without letting on that they were in the area, and get back to him.

YTh@tHussy: HDW dirty

"What the fuck does that mean?" Dalton asked.

"It means I've been compromised," Brycen said through gritted teeth.

YTh@tHussy: Found tracer app. He's tracking your efforts. Whole system is rigged to ping him when his IPs are mapped. Should have known to go through back door by now.

"How was I supposed to know that we were up against a maniac with computer skills? Didn't you say the man was a demolitions expert?" Brycen looked at me.

I'm thinking there's a lot more to Rick I never knew. All I did was nod.

YTh@tHussy: Removed tracer. Built up walls. U should b good.

"How the fuck did she get in?" Brycen asked himself, typing the inquiry.

And that's when Brycen's laptop went dark entirely. As in nothing to display. No power. Zilch! Nada! And my world fell from beneath me.

Brycen immediately began to hit buttons in hopes to power up again when Shane's phone rang. "If she fucked up my system, I swear," he growled. But it hadn't been the case. The damn thing fired up like it should and loaded just fine. "Huh!"

"Detective Peters." The man's eyebrows rose to his hair

line as he pulled his phone from his ears, swiped his finger over the screen, then said, "You're on."

The voice was distorted to be unrecognizable, but the softness to the words, the way this person spoke, had me convinced that this was a woman, never mind the screen name.

"V@por?"

"Who's this?" Brycen asked.

There came a soft, borderline shy laugh. "I shut you down and you've already forgotten about me? I must not be that good."

My patience for formalities and wit was long gone. "Look, whoever you are, my fiancée is the woman in that feed. Tell me you can get Brycen's shit up and running again." Everyone's heads spun to look my way, arched brows questioning that one word I had uttered without a second thought. Problem was, she wasn't officially my fiancée as of yet. Fuck, she might never be if we didn't get to her back soon. Why hadn't I listened to my brother and put a ring on it?

"I know who you are, Lowell," this mystery person said. "I know what you've done. What's been done to you. I even know about the scar you have on your left ass cheek because of a BB gun incident when you were twelve."

"What the fuck?" came as a whisper while a few of the others chuckled.

"I shut Brycen down out of necessity," Mystery Helper continued. "This Rick guy is bating you, Lowell, and your guy Brycen walked right into his trap. If you don't listen up, Morgan's as good as dead once he's moved her."

"She's on the move?"

"No, but she's about to be if you don't pull your heads out of your asses."

CHAPTER 42

I wish I could say I was confident in this *White Hat Hussy* person's assessment of things, but I refused to take any chances and had Shane pull his men back by two blocks, keeping them in wait, but far enough away for Rick to think that we were following his orders. I did agree with our new cohort, though. It was time to pull our heads out of our asses and treat Rick as if he were a complex mission, one we covered every base on. It was clear that thinking of him working alone had us underestimating his capabilities. The man I used to know, or maybe I never did, had changed.

After Brycen's system had failed, he opted to err on the side of caution and work with Hussy, as we'd dubbed her, to find some sort of resolution on getting Morgan back. Suffice to say, I doubted that there was one without giving myself up.

True to his word, Rick contacted me exactly an hour after his last call. "I see that you've listened." The man chuckled. "I thought the law didn't bargain with terrorists."

I growled but quickly forced my ire back. I had to stay rational…in control. "Is that what you are, Rick?"

"Some would call me a peacemaker, brother."

"You're no brother of mine." Shane urged me to get on with the conversation.

"You wound me, Theo."

"What do you want, Rick?"

"Have you ever wondered why your country does what it does?" I hadn't missed his *your*. And apparently neither had Dalton as he mouthed "fucking traitor," all the while wringing his hands as he leaned onto the table, listening to the conversation. "The United States of America, the land of the brave, the proud, the free!" Fuck, did this man have a few screws loose. Now why hadn't I seen any of this before? "It's amazing the bullshit they feed their denizens. I mean, fight for good ol' Uncle Sam. Be the pride and joy of God, man, and country! Ha! Did you not stop to think that maybe you were the terrorists?"

Dalton popped his knuckles, his rage starting to boil over as mine was about to be unleashed if he didn't get to the point.

"You think you're all perfect. Every single raping and murdering one of you." Rick snorts his disgust. "You pillage; you steal—"

I exploded. "Don't act all high and mighty about the sins of war, Donnelly. You were there with us. You're just as guilty of what you accuse. Now get to the fucking point, asshole!"

"You kiss your mother with that mouth? Or better yet, our sweet Morgan? You know I had her first, right?" A pain-filled moan escaped me before I could snuff it out. "She's such a tiny little thing. It's no wonder so many want her, and who am I to deny them?"

What the fuck is he talking about? "Rick, so help me God—"

"Forget Him, Lowell, He can't get you out of this. Now, let's get down to business, since clearly you've lost your sense of fun over the years." *And you've lost your mind, buddy.* "You're going to leave your boys behind, get in a car, and drive. You've got an hour to get to the address I'm about to text you. A minute late, and well…" Rick's voice dropped a few octaves. "Let's just say I'd hate to be Morgan. She's gotten mouthy over the years, and I'm sure you know as well as I do that that mouth of hers can be lethal. It would be a shame to do away with that tongue considering I have a few clients that prefer that to…well, let's just leave it to your imagination shall we?"

The contents of my stomach began to churn. "I want a trade," I uttered without a thought. "Her for me."

Everyone's gaze was on me; heads shaking in refusal with my offer.

Rick's laugh was maniacal. "That's very valiant of you, Theo, but it doesn't work like that."

"The hell it doesn't. This is between you and me." I was becoming desperate here. "Just let her go. You know you don't need her."

"I never thought I'd see the day Sergeant Theodore Lowell would beg," the man said, then paused and I heard my phone chime. "The text is sent. An hour, Lowell, or you'll be collecting pieces of her for the next year by the time I'm done with her. Tick-tock!"

"Rick!" But all I got was a muffled scream of panic right before the line went dead.

CHAPTER 43

My frustration came out in the form of a battle cry. If I didn't need my cell, I'd have smashed it against the wall by now.

Shane's hand met my chest as soon as I turned for the door. "You can't go it alone, man."

"Watch me," I growled. "You have no idea what this fucker is capable of, Shane."

"Let me at least go with you," Dalton pitched in.

As much as I knew it was stupid to go on my own, I wasn't willing to risk Morgan's life. I could barely deal with the terror-filled scream I'd just heard. There's no way I could deal with what could happen between now and the time I reached her, not to mention if I didn't reach her in time, or if I brought company along and Rick found out.

"You know as well as I do you'll need backup." Dalton stood in my face, having pushed Shane back. "It's suicide–"

"It might be, but at least I'll know that she'll be free when I go," I stated.

"No, son." *Dad.* I hadn't realized that he was back from the hospital. The man pushed through the group of men surrounding me.

"Dad, I've got to go."

"If you think I'm letting you out of this house only to lose you when your mother and I have just gotten you back, think again." The desperation in his eyes coincided with his tone. "We've got unfinished business, you and I. I don't know about you, but I sure as hell would like to see things through."

I gave him a curt nod. "Fine. Dalton, pack up all the fire power we've got, then get in the truck. The rest of you are staying put. We'll keep a line of communication open the entire time, but that's as much as I'm allowing. This is my war." Dad's posture relaxed a little. "Tell Mom I love her. I'll be back."

Before I knew it, my father's arms were wrapped around my shoulders, pulling me in. "I'm holding you to that. Now go show that sonofabitch that no one fucks with us Lowells."

It turns out the address Rick texted me belonged to a shipping and storage yard in Newport. Dalton and I were loaded, speeding down the interstate when his phone chimed with a text he promptly opened, then showed me.

"How the hell does she get this stuff?" I asked no one in particular as I looked at an overhead satellite image of the location we were heading toward.

"It's best that you don't ask," I heard Hussy's mechanical voice through my phone, which was set to hands-free.

"Tell me again how you're in this mess with us?" Dalton asked.

"Let's just say I have a lot of time on my hands."

Dalton chuckled. "You do know that most people wouldn't hack into shit to keep busy, right? We hook up with friends, have a few drinks, shoot a game of pool or something."

"I'm not most people, Kip, and for what it's worth, I don't have that luxury." Call me crazy, but I picked up a certain note of envy in her tone.

"Why? You ugly?"

My head snapped in Dalton's direction. "What the fuck, man?"

"What?"

Still, this Hussy character didn't seem aggrieved by my friend's comment. "I wouldn't say that."

"Then why would anyone choose a computer over–"

"You wouldn't understand. I have my reasons, okay?" Hussy's voice grew softer. "I count a total of fifteen cameras all over this yard, Lowell."

Thank you, baby Jesus! We were back to the task at hand. Not that I really minded the distraction my friend and our virtual assistant provided, but what with the lack of time, we needed to make sure we knew what the hell we were heading into.

"They're all on some kind of loop. I can tell you that Rick's hacked into the system. He's definitely watching."

"Any activity over at our initial location?" I asked.

Shane came on the line. "There's nothing going on. I think we were duped, bro. I wish I could tell you for sure, but our one guy got caught by one of the neighbors as he peeked through the window and called it in."

And this is why I wanted to do this alone. "Seriously? You can't get your men to do things right?"

Shane chuckled. "Hey, I work with them, I don't train them, T."

"Alright, Huss," Dalton said, "wave that magic mouse of yours around—what else you got for us?"

"I like you, Kip." She laughed. "You'll be interested to know that the place seems to be somewhat deserted right now. I've got eyes on Warehouse 10, and according to…" Hussy's voice trailed off.

"What?" I urged her. "What's–"

"Fuck!"

"Huss, talk to me," I ordered.

"You'll have company."

"Details," Dalton demanded as Shane said, "I'm sending some guys in."

"No!" I'm not sure who was loudest, but Dalton, Hussy, and I spoke up before Hussy added, "Let me work! I know how this Rick guy works. I've been inside his system all night now and I can guarantee you that he'll know the minute you set someone else on his tail. He knew about the cops right away."

"So you're saying there might be a snitch on the inside?" I asked.

"That, or he's tapping into the radio feeds," she said. "I've got access to his phone records and I'm running a biometric search for keywords based on what information we have on him."

"What about his email?" I heard Brycen ask.

"Thanks, Captain Obvious, but I've already tackled that route. If it were anywhere on his computer, I would have found it by now, and you would know. I'm not an idiot."

Brycen grumbled. "No need to get pissy."

Dalton laughed at this.

I groaned. "Huss, I need the details on everyone, like yesterday."

"Coming up."

Within minutes, Dalton's phone went crazy with alerts. "Shit, T, you're not going to like this."

"Give it to me," I told him.

"Antonio Bandini, also known as the owner to the yard we're heading to."

"Also known as an alleged terrorist and human trafficker with ties to the Middle East," I added. "We've met briefly before on one of my ops. Is there more?"

"The other guy appears to be muscle according to his DMV shot," Dalton states. "Name is Atal Khalil, also known as—"

"Shanks," Shane provided through my phone.

"Yeah, how'd you know?" Dalton asked.

"I've had my fair share of run-ins with that idiot." Shane chuckled. "He's got enough muscle to take a few men down at once, but for all the brawn, he lacks the brain power to go with it. I'll tell you one thing, though, if he gets anywhere near Morgan with a knife—"

Fuck me, but she didn't need a souvenir from that sadist any more than I ever deserved one from my capture. "He'll be wishing he was never born," I growled. "We're ten minutes out. Hussy, anything else I need to know?" Dalton got out of his seat and hunkered down into the floorboards in an effort to remain inconspicuous.

"It's all I've got for you right now. We don't have the luxury of time, so I'm sorry, but if I find anything more, I'll feed it your way."

"Alright." I turned right, onto the Coastal Storage yard drive. "I'm a few minutes out from Warehouse 10. I'm going in silent."

"Don't have to," Dalton said as he rustled into the backpack he had with him and pulled out a tiny black box with a silver latch and grinned. "I've been itching for a good reason to use this shit. Haven't had a mission where I needed to until now." He deposited one of the items in my hand and shoved another one into his right ear. "Com unit," he explained. "Hussy, you think you can tap into this system since you've put our man Brycen out of commission?" Brycen muttered a few choice words.

"Give me the code and we'll be up and running in seconds." Dalton rattled off a series of numbers intermingled with letters. "We're live," she said. "Go ahead and hang up, you'll be able to talk to every one of us."

Disconnecting the call, I hurried to shove the unit in my ear with only fifteen minutes to go on my hour timeline, noticing that it's as if I had nothing in there at all. "We all good?"

"All good, Mr. T." I groaned as Hussy giggled. Dalton's chuckle was halted by a, "You too, Kip."

The man rolled his eyes at me. "I wish she wouldn't call me that."

"I heard that!"

I rolled the truck to a stop by the warehouse, thankful of the load of crates that would work to conceal Dalton's exit, and at the same time, allow me to get out facing the entryway to my final destination. "It's go time."

CHAPTER 44

I wish I could say that I went in guns blazing and rained bullets down on all of their asses, grabbed the damsel in distress, ropes and all, and made a dramatic escape in the nick of time before the whole building went up in smoke. But that's not how it happened. That shit is better saved for books and movies.

Turning off the overhead light inside the truck and leaving my window partially lowered, I paused with my hand on the door handle. "Give me twenty."

Dalton nodded. "Be safe, bro."

"You too." I made to leave the vehicle, leaving the keys in the ignition in case we needed to make a quick getaway.

Dalton would have my six, but to what extent he'd be able to perform his protective duties was beyond me since this place was pretty much wide open. Luckily, it was the middle of the night and there didn't seem to be anyone around like Hussy had told us.

I was a few feet from the warehouse door when I was clubbed in the back of the head and everything went dark, my mind registering the gravel on which I made impact.

Bound to a chair and gagged, Morgan was the first thing I saw when I came to with a start, sitting on the concrete floor with my arms bound at the wrists, my torso secured to a steel pole, and Dalton talking in my ear telling me to give him a sign of life. Bandini and Rick were hunched on either side of her. The Italian had his hands all over her, a look of hunger in his eyes while Rick's mouth was by her ear, whispering God knows what. Whatever it was had her shaking like a leaf she was so petrified.

"Boss?" My head snapped to my right. Shanks.

Both men looked up, Rick moving in behind Morgan. "Looks like I'll have one happy client since our dear Morgan gets to keep that fabulous tongue of hers," he said, bringing about a nasally chuckle from Bandini. "I thank you for that, Theo. You saved me from ruining the merchandise. It would have been a real shame to dispose of her so soon. You see, Antonio here seems to think she's perfect for him."

The man he was referring to stuck his hand inside Morgan's shirt and filled his palm with one of her breasts, licking her cheek. "It's a pleasure seeing you again, Mr. Lowell."

"Get your fucking hands off of her!" I demanded, my body going rigid as I fought to free myself to no avail.

Morgan struggled against her bindings too. The moment her eyes met mine, the dam broke and her tears streamed forth. I mouthed an, "I love you" to which she simply nodded, her eyes begging me to do something.

"Isn't this sweet!" Rick crooned, then looked at Shanks. "You've checked him for weapons?"

"Uh…"

"Oh, for fuck's sake! Do you have any idea who the fuck you're dealing with?"

"He's not getting out of those ropes, Donnelly," Bandini said. "Shanks knows his way around ropes, among other things. I'm sure you remember, Lowell?"

How could I forget? I had a rather jagged souvenir left over from the beefy Middle Easterner right below my ribcage.

Rick snorted. "You better hope you're right. This fucker's been a pain in my ass for too fucking long. It's time he played dead for real."

This set Morgan off. The woman literally growled her fury, fighting her restraints with everything she had to the point that her wooden chair lifted from the concrete floor and slammed back down hard with a crack. The moment she realized that the chair wasn't as solid as she initially thought hit her as soon as it did me.

Rick pushed down on her shoulders to stop any further movement, then whipped out the buck knife that had been sheathed in his belt with one hand, and held the tip not too far from her left eye, while fisting her hair with the other. "Trust me, Morgan, you don't want to know what this thing can do. Now be a good girl and stop fussing, the fun is only beginning."

My woman's gaze met mine with sheer determination as soon as he released her. I gave her a small nod of encouragement. She'd do her part and I would do mine. Since Shanks was as stupid as Shane had stated, all I had to figure was how I could get to the folding knife I had in my back pocket without anyone noticing. *That's if I can move enough.*

"Antonio, my apologies, but I wouldn't be as successful as I've been if I wasn't thorough. I need to check on a few things, mainly make sure that our friend here hasn't been followed before we get down to business. In the meantime, feel free to enjoy the lady and make sure that she'll satisfy you. But don't mark her up beyond bruising." Rick turned and proceeded out of the warehouse, slamming the door in the process. With him gone, all I had to do was figure out a way where Shanks would be away enough from me so he didn't pick up on my intentions.

"What do you think of this little number, Shanks?" Bandini skimmed the back of his hand over Morgan's cheek, ignoring me altogether. Her eyes showed enough revulsion for the both of us. "Rick recommends her highly."

This might be easier than I thought. Shanks left his post and went to inspect Morgan as if she was a new sports car he was tempted to buy. Both men's attention was solely on her. If I was to make an attempt to get to my knife, it would have to be now.

"Aren't you afraid you'll break her?" Shanks asked, taking a long sniff of her hair. "She'd make a delicious pet, regardless."

"Rick said that she was a tough one. Built to last, or some shit," the man said as I shifted sideways enough to push the knife up and out of my back pocket and toward my hand. "It doesn't matter. They all break eventually."

This made Morgan squeak. She struggled against the chair and the rope holding her in place, once more slamming the thing down and making it creak louder. One of the support spindles came loose.

Shanks groaned, grabbing at his cock. "True. Is this one for you, or you selling her? She seems a little wild. I wouldn't mind a hand in training her."

I'll give it to the horny dumbass, he sure did know how to tie knots. It took me a few tries, stilling myself whenever the men would glimpse my way, but I finally managed to get my knife firmly within my grasp. Now if I could only get it open without stabbing myself in the back, I'd be one step closer.

CHAPTER 45

"Fuck!" Dalton's voice came through my earpiece. "He's setting charges, T. You better get the fuck out of there now!"

By then, my hands were a bloodied mess and I'd managed to loosen the ropes around my wrists, but not without jabbing myself in the side with my knife, which hurt like a sonofabitch, and my side felt sticky so I knew it was only a matter of time before one or both men noticed something if they came too close.

Bandini grumbled. "What's taking him so long?"

I was playing with a multitude of scenarios in my mind when the idea to get Shanks away from his boss struck. It was a longshot, but if I could manage the feat, I might be able to free myself in enough time to take Bandini out and get Morgan out of here alive. Then, I'd hunt down Rick and take him apart, limb from limb, like he threatened to do to the love of my life.

Morgan kicked at the loosened support spindle and it went flying across the floor.

"Stop that!" Bandini grabbed Morgan around her neck. She gasped through the gag in her mouth, a gurgling sound coming from her throat, her eyes bulging, chest heaving.

In an effort to take Bandini's focus from Morgan, my mouth kicked into action. "You know you're getting fucked on this deal, right?" Both men turned to me like I hoped. I felt the rope securing my torso give way a bit. I nodded my head toward Morgan. "You know he used to be a demolitions expert with the marines, right? I bet you he's got this place wired and ready. How long do you think before the roof of this place gets blown sky high?"

Shanks seemed worried as his gaze flew between me and his boss, but Bandini maintained his composure, releasing his hold on Morgan as he chuckled. "It's one of the reasons why I sought him out, Lowell. You remember London, don't you?" Oh boy, do I ever. I'd seen the end result of that shipyard explosion. As a matter of fact, it had actually reminded me of Donnelly's work. My eyes narrowed on him and his smirk grew into a grin. "I see that you're only now just discovering the truth. As it is, Donnelly has something I want. It's that simple. He's proven himself quite savvy over the last few years, and as much as I've loved having him as a soldier, I have to say that having him as a business partner has been somewhat beneficial." The leer he threw Morgan's way made me want to vomit.

"Cough once for one, twice for two, T," Dalton's voice comes through again. "You want me to take Rick out or hold him for you?" I coughed three times, hoping he'd get what I meant. His chuckle was a low one. "Got it. He's all yours, but if you're not out in fifteen, I'm having my way with him." I coughed once to let him know I approved. I may have wanted to be the one to take Rick out, but if I couldn't, Dalton would have been my next best choice to do the deed.

"How long have you known him?" I asked. "You said a few years–"

Both men grinned, but Bandini was the one to answer. "About as long as I've known you, Mr. Lowell."

"So why him? Why not me, Antonio? How much are you willing to bet that he's not making off with your cash right now only to take you and Shanks here out of the game permanently?"

Shanks gave a confident laugh. "He'd be crazy to—"

Bandini smirked. "I highly doubt it. He gets no money until I'm in a secure spot and make the call to have the funds wired." I'd say that was sound business practice for a guy in his line of work, but I'd be willing to bet my life on the little fact that their new partner had a few hidden talents that they had yet to know about. "But to answer your first two questions, your friend out there broke within the first hour. I needed a guy, he turned first, so I took him. If you ask me, it was a little too easy. You, on the other hand, is who I wanted. You would have been good, but your refusal to break is what guaranteed you a death. But, then again, we know this next part of the story, right?"

"I bet you were pissed about that, weren't you?"

"Do you have any idea how many millions you've cost me? First in–"

I cut him off with a humorless laugh. "I don't care about your lost millions. You claim to be a prolific businessman, but just as you've failed with each and every time I've managed to infiltrate your little terrorist operations, you've failed yet again." Shanks and Bandini both graced me with confused gazes. "How so, you may ask? Well, let me enlighten you. How close of an eye have you kept on your man Rick since he's turned?" As the big bad boss pondered this, Morgan was making an attempt to kick at the second and final support spindle to her chair. "He's a former US Marine which means he's highly skilled in combat, not to mention he's always been a genius to get himself out of certain situations. But you know this already, we've established that."

Bandini steps closer, his focus completely off of Morgan now. "In my business, being able to weasel yourself out of getting caught is considered a necessity."

"I agree. It's a huge asset. Especially when your newest acquisition is perceived as dead." Then I turned to Shanks. "I have to tell you, Atal, your skill with a knife is legendary. I would know. Even the locals are raving about it!" I grinned when the Italian boss' face flushed red with his rage. "But back to Rick. You're dealing with a ghost, Bandini, and this one in particular knows the ins and outs of making people like you and me, not to mention, Morgan and Shanks over there, disappear, just like he knows how to make himself do the same." I wiggled within my ropes, feeling them give way after having sliced through another two coils. "The only thing, though, is that if any of us four disappear, we'll actually be dead, while he's off God knows where, gallivanting the planet on some rich mob-boss wannabe's dime—because between his capture and now, he's acquired a few interesting talents."

"What the fuck are you talking about," he spat.

"Were you aware of his superior skills with a computer?" The man blanched. "Yeah, surprising right? I was a little shocked myself when I discovered this earlier today."

"You're telling me he's a hacker?"

I gave him a curt nod. "I don't have confirmation on that, but he's got some basic knowledge if he can manage to infiltrate a former FBI agent's system to discover he's being tracked." And that seemed to do the trick.

Bandini turned to Shanks, which gave me enough time to undo the rest of my bindings. "Find Donnelly and bring him back here. It's time he and I had a little chat."

CHAPTER 46

A lot happened in a short amount of time after Shanks left to hunt Rick down. Morgan managed to kick the last support spindle from her chair. All it took to send the thing crumbling was one last hard shove to lift the dilapidated wooden piece of furniture off the floor, slamming herself back down. It wasn't graceful, and it looked as if it didn't come free of pain, but there wasn't any time to worry about that.

Bandini's mistake was turning his back on me to prevent Morgan from escaping. Damn, but that tiny spitfire of mine made me proud.

Fighting the residual hold of the ropes, I managed to pull myself to my feet in time to lunge at the Italian as he wound up to hit her. My hand wrapped around his wrist, wrenching his arm behind his back where I felt the pop in his shoulder. The man cried out like the pussy that he was. Wielding my knife, my other arm rounded his body in a less than stellar grip thanks to the blood coating my hand, pressing the blade up against his jugular.

"You can't hide behind your precious Shanks now, can you?" I spat into the man's ear. "I told you three years ago that you'd suffer if I saw you again. I never saw you, but I sure took pleasure in shutting down some of those operations of yours. I guess you're some masochist begging for more, huh?" Morgan looked entranced yet terrified at the same time as she skittered backwards, away from the products of her confinement. I wished she didn't have to see this side of me at all, but it was inevitable if we wanted to live to see tomorrow.

"P-please!"

"I'm going to do you a favor. Actually, it's not really for you, it's for a buddy of mine, you see?" I dug the knife in a bit more, Morgan's eyes widened at what I pretty much could gather was the sight of Bandini's blood. "If it were up to me, I'd slide this blade through your throat and watch you bleed out. I'd take great pleasure in it, make no mistake about that. But aside from the fact that I've got somewhere to be right now, I'm going to show you mercy where you showed me none. I'll let Jacksonville's finest handle you, then…when you're locked up, I'll let the rest of the men who you've stolen from, framed, and wronged in every other way, take care of you. I'm sure you'll enjoy getting fucked in the ass. After all, isn't rape one of your favorite pastimes, because I sure as fuck know that those girls you've been shipping all over the globe sure as fuck never agreed to your views on slavery."

"I-I–"

I didn't let him finish. Tightening my grip and twisting his bum arm further, I stuck him in his side like the pig that he was, then knocked him over the head with the butt of my knife. I proceeded to drag him to where I'd been restrained, searched him for weapons or anything that could possibly be used to free himself or alert others to come to his rescue, then secured his feet first, then his arms, around the pole at his back by his wrists.

As I got up from my haunches, I turned to face Morgan. Just when I thought she'd be terrified, maybe even repulsed by my actions, she proved to me just what kind of woman she was. With a running leap into my arms, she wrapped her legs around my torso, no care that I was covered in my own and Bandini's blood, or that we were both filthy. Her lips met mine in a hard and all-too-brief kiss. Her body shook with what I was sure was an adrenaline drop.

"I've got you, baby, and I'm never letting you go," I swore.

"What about Rick and Shanks?" She dropped her legs from my waist and I eased her down to her feet.

"T, it would be great if you could join the party here," Dalton shouted in my ear. "Fuck!" I heard a groan and some rustling.

"Dalt?"

"Who are you talking to?" Morgan asked.

I pointed to my ear, tilting my head sideways to show her I had an earpiece, making her eyes widen. "Dalton!" I called again only to be met with more grunts and groans. "I have to get out there. Dalton, where are you?"

"East side…of building." He paused. "Docks. Shanks."

"On my way, bro, but let me get Morgan somewhere safe first." I grabbed Morgan's hand and pulled her toward the door as Dalton grunted his assent. "I want you to get behind the wheel of the truck and get the hell out of here. Get to my brother's. I don't know what I'm going to see when I get to Dalton, but I need to finish this." Opening the driver's side door, I pushed her into the seat. Grabbing her by the back of the neck, I fused my lips to hers in a brief kiss. "I love you, now get out of here."

"I love you too, Theo. Please come back to me."

"You know I will." I forced a smile, releasing her from my grasp. "We have years left together. Now, go!" I slammed the door and ran toward Dalton's location.

As I rounded the south east corner to Warehouse 10, Shanks was proving his namesake by branding a Ka-Bar.

"Shane, you better set the cavalry in motion. Morgan's heading toward you. Send one of our guys to intercept her," I said.

"Already done. Cade and Brycen are on their way to her now," he said as I heard a door slam. "I'm right behind them. SITREP?"

"Bandini is incapacitated and tied up. I'm about to jump in and save Dalton's hide with Shanks." Apparently Dalton didn't appreciate this and seemed to put up more of a fight, as though he was determined to be the one to take the big lug down. For a medically retired Army Ranger, his skill with hand-to-hand was still top notch. Then again, he did own his own security firm, and by that simple fact alone, I doubted he'd let himself off of his former training regime. Hell, he probably demanded that his employees be able to match him just in order to stay employed. "Haven't seen Donnelly since he left the warehouse, but I know he's around here somewhere."

"Hold tight," Shane said. "You'll still have Hussy if you need anything else. Hussy, you still there?"

"I'm your girl, Mr. T. Just let me know what you need."

Chuckling, I pulled my trusty knife out and flicked it open before proceeding slowly toward the scuffling duo. "I've already got one of those, but take your pick of the rest of my guys. They could use someone like you to keep them on the straight and narrow."

As Dalton grunted, sending a kick into Shanks' stomach, making the guy rear back and drop his knife, he said, "Remind me to get busy the next time you're trying to take a guy twice your size down." For a massive lump of muscle, the sonofabitch was quick as he lunged at Dalton's legs, one of them bending at an unnatural angle.

"Dalton, fuck!" I rushed the two scrambling men.

Shane and Hussy both chimed in my ear with, "What?"

I didn't bother to answer, too busy in joining the scuffle by jumping on Shanks' back and arching his neck back in a chokehold. This bullshit was ending now. "It's time to pay the piper asshole," I said as I sliced threw his carotid, the air rushing out of his lungs through his severed windpipe. The man struggled against my hold, as I rolled us over and off of Dalton for a few more seconds, his body twitching before he went limp, the arterial spray ceasing almost immediately.

Rolling Shanks' body off of me, I got to my knees and crawled over to Dalton. The man was sitting there, clutching at his gimp leg as he pulled his jeans up.

"You okay?"

"Not sure." He pulled at his calf holster, grasping his gun only for a gunshot to ring out, the bullet zipping past my ear to snap it out of his hand, bringing forth a pained cry from him.

Several things happened over the next few seconds. I registered Rick holding a smoking gun, a set of headlights, Hussy was yelling in my earpiece along with Shane, and then the crunching of metal against bone, against more metal. And then it was as if time stood still.

It was the incessant blaring of the vehicle's horn that brought me out of my stupor. The blaring horn of Paxton's truck to be exact. And if Paxton's truck was here, that meant—

"Morgan!" I shot up to my feet, an injured Dalton forgotten. Hussy forgotten. The fact that Rick lay sprawled, most of his entrails strewn across the hood of the Dodge Ram…forgotten. The only thing that mattered was getting Morgan away from the wreckage that could possibly cause those charges Rick had lain to blow. I was ten feet from her when her door opened and she tumbled onto the gravel, coughing and grabbing at her midsection.

I grabbed for her arm, rushing to get her to her feet so we could get away from the wreck and most certain doom when she cried out.

"Shit, Morg!" I changed my tactic, picking her up bridal style, rushing us past Dalton toward the docks and set her down on the wooden planks. "I'll be right back, baby. Lay still, I'm going to get Dalton."

The moment I reached him, shoving his arm over my shoulder to help him to his good foot, he chuckled. "Your woman's fucking crazy."

I couldn't help the grin on my face as we hobbled over to where Morgan was. "Brother, her brand of crazy works for me. And it saved our asses. You okay?" I set him down, taking the time to inspect his injuries.

"That's my fucking shooting hand, bro, and the bullet's lodged in my leg." Judging by Dalton's expression, he'd heard the girly gasp through our com units. "I'm fine, guys," he said then nodded his head toward Morgan. "Go tend to your woman."

Getting to my knees, I turned toward her, disliking the sheen of sweat that now coated her face. It wasn't exactly that warm out tonight. "Baby, what hurts?"

She reached out an arm and I helped her sit up as she clutched her side with the other. "Shit! Fuck!"

"Baby, tell me what hurts and I'll make it better."

"My ribs. I think I might have busted something when I hit the steering wheel," she explained.

"I've got an ambulance on the way," Hussy said before I had to ask. "Dalton, are you sure you're—"

"You're going to want to send in a bomb squad and fire crew too, if this place goes up," I told her.

"Uh…okay. On it."

"And Huss?" I could feel my emotions getting the better of me now that the worst was over. Careful not to jostle Morgan too much, I sat close to her, wrapping an arm around her shoulders. She settled her head against my chest.

"Yeah?"

Swallowing the lump in my throat, I croaked a, "Thank you." Those two words were far from enough, but they were all I had right now.

I guess emotions were running high for everyone as her voice came out at a whisper. "You're welcome, Mr. T."

Dalton spoke next. "Huss?"

"Yeah?"

"I'll be fine." His voice was gravelly. "But I am going to need your name, honey."

A real voice came through, breathless and definitely that of a woman's. "Kip…"

Dalton sucked back surprised air. "I want to know—"

"Don't." She sounded exhausted, beaten even. Not that she wasn't before, but without the voice distorter, she became real to me, and I think Dalton felt it too, if not more.

"Let's just leave it at this. I only did what needed to be done. It's what I do."

Dalton's eyes met mine. "Okay, Huss," he whispered. "If you ever need anything–"

"I won't." The line went silent for a moment. "But tell you what, I'll be in touch if something ever comes up."

"Okay."

"I'm going to sign off now."

"Huss?" Dalton called out, his voice holding a subtle note of desperation. Nothing came through but static. Hussy was gone. And the cavalry had arrived.

CHAPTER 47

Morgan hissed for what seemed like the zillionth time as I reached for my cell phone which I'd managed to scour from my brother's floorboards prior to jumping in the ambulance. Paxton picked up on the first ring.

"Tell me you've got Morgan. We just got home and Dad's the only one here. He said everyone left in a tizzy but never explained anything. Is she okay? How're the guys? What's going on?"

"She's fine. We're heading to the hospital. She might have a few cracked ribs, but I don't think it's anything serious."

"And Rick?"

"That's a whole other story." I huffed out a dry laugh. "He and your truck are long gone."

"You wrecked my truck?"

"Nah, you've got Morgan to thank for that." The woman groaned, her hand squeezing mine, her fingernails digging into my flesh. "Easy girl!"

She growled. "He was going to kill you both, what else was I supposed to do?"

"You were supposed to let me handle things and get the fuck out."

"You're welcome." Christ, she was adorable when she pouted.

Paxton's heartfelt laugh warmed me. He'd clearly heard our exchange. "Tell her that I don't care about the truck."

"I will. Listen, we're just pulling up to the hospital now,

can you let everyone know that Dalton's been shot, but aside from Morgan and him, we're all okay?"

"You know I will. And T?"

"Yeah."

"I know you haven't put a ring on it yet. The box is sitting on my kitchen table. What the hell are you waiting for?"

"About that…" Morgan's confused gaze met mine and I was thankful that I hadn't pressed the speakerphone option.

"You don't want to wait any longer, do you?"

"Fuck, no!" spilled out of me in one breath.

"Okay, I'll meet you there as soon as I reassure everyone."

"Thanks, bro." Hanging up, I leaned over and kissed Morgan. "I love you."

The pain in her face eased a bit as a look of serenity filled it. "I love you too, Theo." Dalton groaned in his seat, his hand and leg bandaged to staunch the bleeding, an IV in his healthy arm. "And Dalton?"

"Yeah?" His head was tilted back against the ambulance wall, his jaw tight from pain and his eyes were shut.

"I think I might love you just a little bit too. Thanks for having my man's back." Her voice quivered and a tear spilled over, my hand automatically reaching to brush it away.

He looked down at Morgan, his face suffused with a blush I'd never seen before, boring an awe-shucks-ma'am expression, his usual hard gaze softening. "I'd do it again, if I had to."

I spoke what I knew he saw in my eyes when his gaze landed on me. "The feeling's mutual, brother, but let's hope it never comes to that."

Tilting his head back and closing his eyes once more, he grunted.

CHAPTER 48

After being poked, prodded, and run through an x-ray machine, the doctor had come in to inform us that Morgan had sustained bruising to her ribs. She'd have some swelling and pain for the next little while, but we'd been assured that with lots of rest and some medication, she'd be good as new within a few weeks, if not sooner.

Shortly thereafter, the nurse came in with her discharge papers, a prescription for pain killers, and bound her up to help ease some of the discomfort.

We crashed hard after settling in at Paxton's in the early hours of the night. Hell, I don't think I've slept that many consecutive hours since I was a teenager.

Turning to my side, I found Morgan still sleeping soundly, thanks to the pain medication we'd picked up on our way home.

As I lay there beside her, a day after our ordeal being over, the ring I held in my hand weighed heavily.

It's time.

Reaching for her left hand, I slid my ring over her finger. The fit was perfect, just like she was. Depositing her hand over her stomach, my fingers sought out a path of their own, starting at her hairline. I traced her brows, the taped gash on her cheek, down the bridge of her nose, to her smiling pout.

"What are you doing?" she whispered, her voice husky from sleep, her eyes still closed.

My fingers moved to trace her dainty jawline. "I need to touch you, to know that this is real."

Morgan's eyes opened and those chocolate pools of hers bore into mine. "Baby?" Her hand came up to cup my cheek. "Is everything—" On a gasp, her hand snapped back, eyes starting to glisten. "Theo?"

"It's time we make it official, don't you think?" I hovered closer to her, kissing away the first stray tear. "I meant to give it to you at the cabin, but I kept waiting as if the perfect moment would come to me. I shouldn't have. You know why?" She shook her head. "Because every moment with you is perfect." I grabbed her hand, kissing the ring that sat atop it. "Every day is precious. You're my heart, Morgan. I'm damn lucky that I found you."

"No, *I* found *you*. After all, I did ask you to plug up my hole." She smirked.

I shrugged. "Potato, patato." This caused both of us to laugh. "Morgan?"

"Hmm?"

"Tell me again that you'll marry me." I nuzzled her nose with mine. "Let me be your love, your happiness, your family—"

"My hero too?"

I could no longer dispute her view of me. After yesterday, we'd both earned that title. She was mine, as I was hers. "That too."

Her smile brightened her entire face. "I'd be honored to have you as my husband, Sergeant Lowell. But on one condition." She wrapped her free hand behind my neck and pulled me closer, her lips skimming mine.

"Tell me and it's yours, baby."

"Get rid of that Mr. T doll?"

"Sure." I agreed without really realizing what she'd said. "Hold on, what?" I reared back to see if she was serious.

"The Mr. T doll that's on the dresser."

I turned toward the piece of furniture in question and found the mint condition action figure in its box, a small cream envelope attached to it. "Who brought that?"

"Don't know. I noticed it there earlier when I went to the bathroom. You were still sleeping."

I jumped out of bed to fetch the card.

I pity the fool! You may be white and a hell of a lot more handsome, but you'll always be my Mr. T. I hope you live a lifetime of happiness with Morgan. Congratulations!—Hussy

"Who's it from?" Morgan asked as a laugh boomed out of me when it all sunk in.

"Hussy."

CHAPTER 49

Apparently, I hadn't been the only one to have been targeted by our little hacker girl. Later that day, Morgan and I headed to the hospital to spend some time with Dalton, despite my insistence that she stay home and rest.

My fiancée gasped as soon as we entered. "Wow, Dalton, are you doubling as a florist now?"

That had me doubling over, laughing.

"Yeah, yeah. Laugh all you want." Although he behaved disgruntled, the man's complexion had taken a pink hue.

"Hussy?" I asked.

His eyes softened. "Yeah."

There was something special about that little lady, and if I wasn't mistaken, Dalton seemed rather charmed by her.

"I want to meet this Hussy person," Morgan said as she claimed the chair closest to Dalton's bedside after kissing his cheek. The man and I looked at each other.

"Sweetheart, I don't think that'll happen."

"Why not?"

"We never got her real name," I explained.

"We tried, but…" Dalton looked toward the room's window and kind of floated off into a world of his own making.

"Didn't you say that Brycen can hack into computers?" I nodded and Dalton's head snapped back to look at her, eyes wide. "Couldn't you get him to, I don't know, get on his computer and follow some kind of reverse path from how she connected to him the last time, and then get to her?"

"Trust me, I've been trying. It's not that easy." Brycen came into the room, foul mood apparent. "That damn girl! I swear, I am going to find her and when I do, she's going to wish she never messed with me. Fucking dancing babies."

I laughed. "You just can't take the fact that you were bested by a girl."

"Maybe," he paused. "But whenever I think I have a lead on her, I'm left to deal with bald-headed little trolls prancing around my screen in diapers."

Morgan harrumphed as I said, "Tell us how you really feel."

The guy gave me a perplexed look. "You just don't get it! You don't mess with another hacker's shit."

"Of course you do!" Morgan said. "Isn't that what you do? You find holes in walls or whatever and sneak into databases and find information? Isn't that all part of making programs better? If you do that with systems, why couldn't you do it to other hackers?"

"She's got you there, Bryce," I said.

"So you haven't found her?" Dalton asked.

"She's somewhere in this area, that much I know." Dalton nodded in understanding. "What's it to you?" The man just shrugged, but didn't elaborate. "I have to hand it to her though, she's good. If I knew where she was, I'd be on you to offer her a job, Dalt."

"So find her," Morgan said as if it was the simplest thing.

"Haven't you been listening, woman?" Brycen looks over at me. "Theo, I said I'd love your woman, but man, I'm not liking her all that much right now."

Morgan reached for his hand and pulled him to her side, making him nudge me out of the way as she did so. The man bent toward her. Kissing his cheek, she patted his other one and said, "Thank you. Theo told me everything that happened while Rick had me. I know you worked to get me back. You might wish that you had a more active role, but I'm back, and you're part of the reason that I am. From what I hear, you're one of the best at what you do. You weren't the only one to underestimate Rick's capabilities. And I also happen to know that you'll manage to trip her up at some point, because you're that good." Brycen's eyes softened when she pecked his cheek a second time and gave him a bright smile, her hand finally letting go of his.

"Awe, fuck." He straightened and looked at me. "It's a good thing you're keeping her, T, because I'd be tempted to change my ways and make this one mine."

An hour later, Shane joined us over his lunch break. The man scrubbed a hand at the back of his neck, a sigh escaping him as his ass found a chair.

"What's up with you?" I asked.

Shane grumbled and then fixed his eyes on Brycen. "Did you have to send me all that evidence?"

"What evidence?"

"Those cold case files I sent over last month, the ones Dalton's got you working on," he explained.

"I haven't–" Brycen's eyes widened as one word summed it all up. "Hussy!"

CHAPTER 50

Whithen dawn broke, as with every morning since all hell had broken loose with Morgan's and Jasper's capture, I found myself indulging in one of life's simplest of things: the sight of my better half laying asleep beside me.

It'd been six months since Rick had met his death, two months since Antonio Bandini was sentenced and put in prison, and a month since we'd finished turning Morgan's home into the home she'd always dreamed of having, arguments and make-up sex included. She may have gained in the way of construction knowledge, but after six months of working together, when someone refers to a screwdriver as a "doo-hickey", a wrench as a "doo-dad", or every other tool as a "thing-a-ma-bob", I have to resign myself that my soon-to-be-wife would be somewhat hopeless when it came down to my job. Then again, the same could be said about me with regards to her floral business. What the fuck was baby's breath anyway?

"Good morning." Morgan's sleep-hazed voice knocked me back to the present. She twisted her body to lay on its side, her front pressed against mine.

"Good morning, baby." I nuzzled her nose. "All set for today?"

The twinkle in her eyes, the wide smile was answer enough. "I've been ready since you asked me." Wrapping her hand behind my head, she pulled me in for a lazy kiss. Her intent became clear as soon as she rubbed her breasts against my chest, curving her upper leg over my hip.

Her attempt at taking things up a notch by sneaking her

other hand down between our bodies toward my fully erect cock was brought to a halt as I reached for her wrist and deposited a soft peck to her lips. "We can't, baby."

She looked pained, and to be honest, I was feeling it too. "Theo, this is ridiculous. We fucked just last night."

Rolling her to her back, I smiled down at her, covering her body with mine. "It's only for a few more hours."

She sighed, her eyes searching mine. "You're serious." It wasn't a question.

"I am." I began to trail my lips from her cheek down toward her chin, following the edge of her jaw to her neck. "But I definitely can be persuaded..." I pulled one of her nipples into my mouth and sucked hard, "to relieve some of your tension..." I repeated the act on its twin, "in a *tasteful* manner."

Her back arched high on a moan, her hands directing my head where she wanted it most. "Please, Theo."

Shimmying down her body, I bent her legs at the knees and spread her wide. The sight of her glistening had me salivating. "You're dripping, Morg."

"I don't know what it is lately, but just the thought of you has me in a state of perpetual arousal," she confessed.

This made me grin. "Really?" I blew a puff of air, her pussy clenching.

"Uh-huh!"

"When did–"

On a huff, she leaned up on her elbows and looked down at me with a frustrated look. "Theo, if you're not going to shut up and fuck me with that tongue of yours, I swear you'll be sleeping on the couch on our wedding night," she growled.

She let out a keening cry as I ran my tongue up the length of her dripping folds. "We can't have that, can we?" Introducing a finger, feeling for that sweet spot of hers that was sure to make her detonate, I went to work.

It had only been five hours since I'd left her with the girls, but I was pacing like a caged animal chomping at the bit to see Morgan again.

"Nervous?" Paxton entered the room, closing the door behind him.

"Not at all."

The man's smile widened. "Ah, I get it. You're impatient."

I let out a loud sigh. "Like you wouldn't believe. Remind me again why I said yes to this whole big wedding thing?"

At that moment, Dalton entered the room, dressed in his formal Army dress and grinned. "It's time."

Finally!

CHAPTER 51

Spring had sprung and all around, everything around me was thriving. I sat on our back patio and watched over Morgan as she went about, tending one of her many gardens. Just the sight of her had me smiling.

"How's she been feeling?" Dalton asked. I hadn't seen him in a month due to a job he'd been on, but when I turned to look at him, I caught the wistful look on his face as he watched my wife work.

"Better now that she's in her second trimester. Her morning sickness has tapered off and her energy is back." I couldn't help the grin.

Dalton chuckled. "I bet you're loving that." He took a swig of his beer.

"Mmm," I mumbled as I tilted my bottle back. "So what's new with you?"

The man sighed and leaned his head onto the back of the chair he sat in. "I've got another contract coming up."

"Anything good?"

"I'm heading North to Canada, and then to Mexico," he announced, looking down to his hands. "I could really use your help on this one though, brother." His gaze met mine, the look he was sporting was a somber one.

"What's going on?"

"I was contacted a week ago by some politician up in Ottawa. The member of parliament in question has a son who's been making waves in the news as of late due to a drug habit. The man's fiancée disappeared while they were off on a trip to Mexico."

"Shit, are you talking about Minister Wentworth?" My eyes sought out Morgan, who had dropped her gloves and had gotten to her feet with her bucket of weeds, proceeding toward the back of her barn where I'd set her up with a new composting station shortly after we'd moved back into the house.

Dalton nodded. "Yeah."

I had heard about this case. It had made headlines here in the States since Wentworth was Canada's Minister for Foreign Affairs, but also because of the nature of his woman's disappearance. It was clear that foul play was involved. The politician's son was the main suspect, despite him being found passed out from near-lethal cocaine amounts in his bloodstream. He'd been covered from head to toe in blood; blood that had been proven to belong to his soon-to-be stepmother.

"So, why you?" I asked him, Morgan reappearing, her face, arms, and hands rinsed off.

"Turns out he's got some family ties in the area." The moment my wife had reached me, I made a grab for her, settling her on my lap with one arm around her, and the other surrounding her small but noticeable baby bump. "Wentworth said that I'd worked a case with a relative of his, but for the life of me, I have no clue who the hell he means since he refused to give me a name."

"Wentworth?" Morgan asked.

"Yeah, Dalton here's been asked to look into the politician's woman's disappearance," I caught her up before turning my attention back to my friend. "But you do background checks on everyone you work with, don't you?"

He nodded. "It would be suicide if I worked with people I couldn't trust. Hell, I even ran checks on Bryce and Cade before they started to work for me." My eyes widened at this. "Yeah, I know…but after what you've been through with Rick, what I've been through that landed me with my medical discharge," he growled the last, "can you blame me?"

I suppose I couldn't. This was his business, his livelihood. I'd probably do the same thing if I were in his place. Hell, I'd even paid him to run checks on a few of the guys I've hired as foremen since *TL Construction & Engineering* had taken off.

"Maybe he meant that you handled a case for one of his relatives?" Morgan pondered aloud. Maybe she was right.

"That's what I thought too, but I had Brycen look into things and he hasn't been able to find anything. Wentworth slipped and I know that we're dealing with a female, but that's about it."

"How long will you be gone for this time?" I asked him.

"Gone? You mean you're leaving again already?" I kissed Morgan's temple. I absolutely loved the concern this woman had for my family and friends. I couldn't wait for our child to be born. She'd be the best mother; I just knew it.

"I don't know how long I'll be gone for," he said. "I'm meeting up with Wentworth in Ottawa on Tuesday. Depending on the information I get, I might be coming back to pack up and ship off to Mexico right away."

"You're going alone?" I asked.

"I am." Morgan's body tensed over my lap with this news. "I'd bring Cade along, but his team is in charge of training the new SAR recruits. Brycen can do everything from here, and the others, well, they're only part-timers." He ran his hands through his dark brown hair. "I need to get some new blood in. A few full-time guys that have our kind of training and are willing to go outside the US to do their jobs, especially if contracts like Wentworth's start coming in."

"I don't like this one bit." Morgan bit down on her lower lip, eying the both of us. "We've been watching the news and keeping up with what's going on. Going to Canada is one thing, Dalton, but heading to Mexico when you already know that drugs are involved and…and don't get me started on the other gross details of this case." She shook her head vehemently. "No, it's too dangerous to go at it alone."

"Baby…" Morgan was getting herself worked up about

this, and to be honest, I wasn't thrilled about Dalton's plan either.

Morgan turned to me. "Do you remember what you told him in the ambulance ride from the warehouse?" I nodded. "As much as I don't like the idea of both of you being gone, I know that having both of you working together would be safer."

"What are you saying, Morgan?" Dalton asked.

"She's granting you your wish, Dalton." The man looked confused. "I told you once that I had your back, and I meant it. I don't like the idea of you heading off to Mexico and going it alone about as much as she does. I don't have any new jobs lined up for at least another month, and now that I have foremen that can look after things, I can spare some time."

Dalton snorted before finishing off his beer and getting up to fetch another one from the ice bucket that Morgan had set up for us shortly after my friend's arrival. "Gee, thanks, Mom."

"Toss me another too, while you're at it."

"Got a water there for me, Dalton?" Morgan asked.

"Sure do, pretty–" Dalton's words halted by the doorbell.

"I've got it." Morgan got up to head for the front door.

Handing me my beer and setting my wife's bottle of water down beside my seat, he eyed me up and down. "Are you sure about this?" he asked. "I know I said that I could use you, and it's true, but you've got a pregnant wife here at home. I know Brycen can handle himself out in the field, I could always get him to come with me."

"You're not leaving me behind, and if Morgan has it her way, you can bet your ass that Brycen will be on that flight out to Mexico with us, too. I wouldn't put it past her to get Shane to finally use some of his holiday time and make sure he's with us." I chuckled at the imagery. My beautiful tiny spitfire of a woman sure had all of us wrapped around her little finger.

Dalton, smirked. "Yeah, she's that crazy, but I think that's why we all love her, bro."

Morgan's panicked shriek tore through the stillness of the afternoon. "Theo!"

Dalton and I got to our feet and rushed the house, only to come to a dead halt in front of Morgan, who had some woman sprawled on the floor, her head in her lap.

"What the fuck?" Dalton said as I crouched down beside the duo on the tiled entryway.

Morgan's eyes were wide. "She was just standing there one minute, and then the next, she collapsed into my arms. She's burning up, Theo."

"I'll call 911." Within seconds, I had my cell in my hand, doing just that, watching as Morgan wiped the beads of sweat off the woman's forehead while Dalton rushed to the kitchen, only to come back with a bottle of water and a damp cloth.

"Here, I'll do it." Morgan ripped the cloth from Dalton's hands and immediately started dabbing it over her face and neck while the man began to pace.

The sigh of relief the woman emitted was quickly followed by words that made me blanche. "Mr. T."

I heard it, I know Morgan had too as she looked at me wide-eyed, and Dalton froze right where he was. "W-what, did she say?" Dalton collapsed to his knees beside all of us and studied the unconscious stranger before us.

"Danger…Kip," she managed, and then all was silent.

Dalton's hand gently cupped the woman's cheek as he whispered what I already knew. "Huss?"

EPILOGUE

I was tired, filthy, and stunk to the high heavens of the swamp and jungle, but getting off of that plane and setting foot on Jacksonville soil a week after I'd left, invigorated me. I didn't care that my truck would need a full detailing after riding in it. I just wanted to get home, find my woman, feel her in my arms as her presence erased all of the bad I had witnessed in such a short amount of time and fill me with her light.

I rolled up the drivewayslowly, taking in my home and saw a head peeking up over a bundle of rosebushes as I parked my truck. It didn't take but two seconds before I saw Morgan throw her sheers up behind her and started making a run for me, gardening gloves, rubber boots, dirt-smudged cheeks, a mint green sundress, and all. The second my feet hit the gravel out of my truck, I sprinted forward, catching her as she leapt with an excited shriek into my arms, fusing her lips to mine.

"Oh, God, you reek!" Morgan actually gagged, but her arms had yet to loosen their grip, and so did the two legs that were now wrapped around my waist. "Where the hell have you been? Why didn't you call when you landed? I would have–"

I slammed my lips back onto hers and pulled away. "Shut up, woman," I growled. "Please tell me that you're done for the day. I haven't seen or spoken to my wife in a week, I've barely slept because I worried about her and our baby, I've been told I reek, which means I need to hose myself down before thinking about going into my house to take a shower and spend the rest of the day sinking myself deep inside my wife to remind her of how much I love her."

A throat cleared behind us with Morgan giggling into my shoulder. "So I guess we're done for today?" a voice I recognized immediately said.

I turned around and grinned. "Well if it isn't our little Hussy!"

The woman blushed. "You can stop calling me that now that you know my name, Theo."

"You'll always be Hussy or Huss to us, Devolin," I told her.

She nodded, looking down at her feet. "I'm glad you're back safe," she whispered. I could see the wheels turning in her head, knew that she was fighting the urge to ask me how the rest of the team was, caring more for one particular member than the others. "I-I guess I should get going. Morgan, give me a call if you need me." Meeting my gaze, she forced a smile and then turned to leave.

"Hey Dev?" She turned to acknowledge me. "He's okay." A look of relief entered her features, but as soon as it appeared, a wall of indifference took its place. She waved and then proceeded to jump into her car, driving off. Still holding Morgan in my arms, I squeezed her ass in my hands before lowering her back down to the ground, my lips brushing hers softly. "Head on into the house and get the shower warmed up. Give me a couple of minutes to hose the jungle off of me, and I'm all yours, baby."

Watching those hips of hers sway as she walked off had my imagination running on hyper drive with ideas of what I wanted to do to her when I got inside.

Leaving my soiled clothes in a heap by the back door, I

made my way through the house and into our bedroom in nothing but my birthday suit. The steam in the air hit me as soon as I entered the bathroom, and so did the low moans.

The sight of my woman through the glass enclosure, leaning back against the tiled wall facing me as she pleasured herself had me groaning. "Fuck, Morg, you're killing me here." To show her how she affected me, I grabbed my cock and gave it a few hard strokes.

"Why don't you hurry that sexy ass of yours up and come and join in on the fun."

She didn't have to tell me twice. In two strides, I was opening the door to let myself in. She made to reach for me but I shook my head. "No. Keep playing with yourself, baby. I want to see all of you." I licked my lips.

"But–"

I took myself in hand and her eyes darted down to my crotch. She moaned. "Don't worry about me just yet." I lowered myself to my knees, continuing to stroke myself slowly as I bent enough to nuzzle her pubic bone with my nose, then lifting my head enough to drop a kiss onto her belly, which seemed to have popped out even more during my absence. "You're so sexy, Morg." I released myself, putting my hands on her hips and meeting her hooded gaze. "Tell me, are you ready for me?"

"Always," came out breathlessly as her fingers thrust into her heat, her thumb circling her clit.

"Good," I growled. "Don't get yourself off just yet, baby. Your orgasms belong to me."

Life didn't get any sweeter than this. Aside from scrounging a little sustenance for dinner, Morgan and I had yet to leave the bedroom. Now, the sun was setting on the horizon and she was cocooned in my arms, our baby bump wedged between us.

That's when I felt it.

That first kick, which had my body going stiff. Then the

second one. That one had me tightening my hold on Morgan as I buried my head in her neck, my body beginning to shake, my eyes burning behind their closed lids.

Morgan's grip on me tightened. "Baby, what's wrong?"

I couldn't open my mouth to say anything for fear of breaking down, but a moment later, it happened anyway.

"Theo?" Morgan's voice quivered. "Baby, you're scaring me. What's gotten into you?"

Taking a deep breath to control the tears that were now free falling against Morgan's shoulder, I rolled her onto her back, cradled her face in my hands, and pressed a tender kiss on her lips before whispering, "Thank you."

"Theo, what's—"

"You've given me so much more than I could have ever imagined," I told her. "I thought I knew that already, I thought I'd let go of everything in my past that made me hold on to the guilt, but it wasn't until just now that I felt truly at peace with my decision to move on."

"Oh, baby." She pulled me to cradle my head against her chest.

That night, I couldn't sleep. It wasn't because of worry, but because of excitement. In my arms I held my best friend, my love, my whole world—my life.

When I'd come back to Jacksonville and met Morgan for the first time, I'd felt vindicated in my belief that settling wasn't the way to go. But she'd proven me wrong about that, and in so many other ways.

Now I knew that my way of thinking was what it was—a ploy of self-preservation. Morgan made me a better man. She made me happy. She made me stronger. She healed parts of me I never thought would ever get better.

But despite all that, there was one thing that had eluded me, until tonight, that is. Despite my numerous blessings, I still couldn't bring myself to feel as if I deserved everything that was thrust upon me over these last fifteen months. Feeling those kicks seemed to have knocked me to my senses, though. That one last missing piece to my life's puzzle clicked right into place.

In Morgan I had found my salvation. But in the life we'd created together—therein lay my redemption. What more could this marine ever ask for?

ABOUT THE AUTHOR

Born and raised in small town Northern Ontario, Canada, Carey Decevito has always had a penchant for reading and writing.

More than a decade later, with weeks of sleepless nights, where exhaustion settled into her everyday existence, she finally gave in and put pen to paper (more like fingers to keyboard!) She submitted to the dreams that plagued her. And the rest, as they say, is history!

A member of the RWA, Carey Decevito enjoys spending time with family and friends, the outdoors, traveling, and playing tourist in Canada's National Capital region. When life gets crazy, she seeks respite through her writing and reading. If all else fails, she knows there's never a dull moment with her prolific storyteller of a daughter, her goofy husband, cat and dog who she swears are out to get her.

Almost Forgotten is the second book in The Broken Men Chronicles series.

FIND CAREY AT:

www.careydecevito.com
carey.decevito@gmail.com

ALSO BY CAREY DECEVITO

The Broken Men Chronicles series:

Once Written, Twice Shy
Almost Forgotten
Play Me to Infinity
To Forgive & Hold Safe
A Heart's War